I0674534

Pulse
Issue 2023-24
The Literary Magazine of Lamar University

Department of English and Modern Languages

LITERARY PRESS
LAMAR UNIVERSITY

Acknowledgements

This edition of *Pulse* was made possible by the generosity of donors to Lamar University. The editors wish to express sincere gratitude to Mrs. Sue Gilbert Mellard for her generous contribution, to Dave Oliphant for his generous contribution that made the cash prizes possible, and to the Department of English and Modern Languages for their continued support of all forms of literary expression. We also thank those who submitted to *Pulse* and appreciate the diligence of our readers and editors. We especially thank Theresa Ener and Katherine Hoerth who made this edition possible.

Pulse Staff

Awards

Eleanor Award for Undergraduate Poetry
"Bedmaking" — Zoë Landers

Sanderson Award for Fiction
"Countdown" — Christine Osborne

Rowe Award for Scholarly Essay
"Intellectual Filth: Nazification and Resistance at the University of Munich" — Brandon Stumpf

Oliphant Award for Poetry in Translation
"The Widest Road" — trans. by Jo Youngeun

Best of Art
"Fake Flowers" — Erica Callahan

Contents

Special Dedication: Dave Oliphant

Poetry

Poetry in Translation

Creative Prose

Scholarly Essays

Biographies

Special Dedication: Dave Oliphant

On *Pulse*
From Dave Oliphant

Sometime in 1958 or '59, a classmate at South Park High School introduced me to the classical music of Charles Ives (1874-1974), a New England composer ahead of his time. I was so enthused by Ives's very American but experimental sounds, based often on hymns and traditional songs of the day, that I acquired and read the first biography of the composer by fellow composer Henry Cowell. In late 1959, it was announced that *Pulse*, a new student literary magazine at then Lamar Tech, was seeking contributions for its inaugural issue. I decided to write an essay on Ives and submit it for publication. Its acceptance by the student editors was one of the most thrilling experiences of my life. Having been recognized by my peers for a piece of writing worth publishing was, without my knowing it, the beginning of a lifetime as a writer. In late 1962, after finally finishing my B.A. degree, I submitted to *Pulse* my poem entitled "An Afternoon of Debussy," which to my surprise was chosen as the winner of the issue's Eleanor Weinbaum poetry award. The three English professors who served as the judges were none from whom I had taken classes, so that their choice of my poem was especially meaningful to me. Charles Ives had written that "prizes are for mediocrity," and Nicanor Parra, the self-styled Chilean "antipoet," had written that "prizes are for friends of the jury." In 2011 I would win the book translation award from the Texas Institute of Letters for my version of Parra's *Discursos de sobremesa* (rendered in English as *After-Dinner Declarations*). Despite critiques of the value or legitimacy of prizes from two of my favorite creative figures, I remain grateful to those who adjudged my writing and translating worthy of the distinction of winning the Weinbaum and TIL awards. As an antipoet, Parra naturally ridiculed the unfairness of prizes, and yet one of his five declarations was delivered to an audience that came to honor him as the winner of the Mexican government's Juan Rulfo award, valued at one hundred and fifty thousand dollars. As for Ives, he belatedly received the Pulitzer Prize in 1947, for music composed three decades earlier. What I want to say about my early essay on Ives and my poem titled after Claude Debussy's *Prelude to the Afternoon of a Faun* is that ever since my two publications in *Pulse*, much of my writing both in prose and poetry has involved music, primarily jazz and classical. The encouragement that those early appearances in Lamar's student literary magazine gave to my career "has made," as Frost has said, "all the difference." For this reason, I am a great believer in the positive impact that a publication like *Pulse* can bring to writers, translators, editors, and readers, as well as illustrators and designers. Two final notes: largely as a result of having been published in *Pulse*, I became in 1964-65 the graduate editor of *Riata*, the student literary magazine of the University of Texas at Austin. Today I am still reading about Ives, having discovered other biographies of the composer and many CDs with commentaries on his still avant-garde music.

An Afternoon of Debussy

Dave Oliphant

1962 Eleanor Award for Undergraduate Poetry

In sleep
he faces
feeling
not seeing
the cracked ceiling
his head
lying at rest
on the soiled pink
pillowcase
her arm extended
beneath the curve of his neck
the baby of five days
reaching its happy hand
toward his rising
sinking chest

Dressed merely by their child
and the pink sheet
crumpled
from waist to knees
her slender feet
cross in anxiety
ankle on ankle
pale
at the foot of the bed

Half-naked
he daydreams
of two young sparrows
mates in the
breast-high grass
bowing their heads
this way and that
keeping feathered ears
in touch
with signals of the palsied
wind
in warning
shaking limbs
of a red-&-yellow
Chinese tallow

Sea horses swim
where waves of leaves
mesh
with a soft blue sky
the view inviting
silent eyes
to enter
the tint of the deep
for there pervades
a flaming mouth:
round
a cymbal ringing
through a music
pure
filled with the breath of
life
floating like bubbles
blown from soap
tilting and
by the
      golden tongue
of the sounding sun
glistened
        pink & blue

        breathe
    o sonorous strings
        sweep horses
    out to sea

        disarm
    French horns
        the hidden fear
    spread in wings

        readied for flight
    should gleaming notes
        burst
    on the wind in the tree

The child
upon their double base
now plays
the feeding tune

elbowing
vibrating
his manly wire-like hair
waking at last
his bright blue eyes
on fire

María's Mask
Dave Oliphant

each night she slips
its white elastic band
over her head &

against her now gray
hair with in its
blue-green satin finish no

slits for eyes not
to masquerade nor to
hide & go unrecognized

but to keep from
being awakened through curtain
or blind by the

peeping moon streetlight or
my over-bright Texas sun
for when she is

she can't fall back
asleep & must read
or arise & begin

her chores even at
four a.m. although has
yet to come to

earplugs against my snores
when I roll over
onto my back or

turn to her side
to blow like a
breaching whale disrupts her

beauty rest her dreams
I'll never sound her
deepest self have never

known can only spy
her lovely lips produce
her Chilean tones whistled

Beethoven or Dylan tunes
or early music for
Arabian oud & once

it's removed the eyes
revealed always steal &
harpoon my heart again

Poetry

Blind Truth
Esveiri Arteaga

When I look into their eyes,
I see innocence and purity.
They swirl their paintbrush,
Mesmerized by the bright and vibrant colors.
That's how the world should be seen through their eyes,
Like a bright and colorful painting.
They are too innocent to understand the violence and corruption
They are really surrounded by.
As they are in their classrooms learning to count,
Others are taking shelter from missiles and bombs.
They don't fully understand,
But there will be a day where they will be
Exposed to everything with no filter.
There will be nothing to shield their eyes,
All the lies they've been told,
The ugly truth will be brought to the surface.
They will realize not everyone has a reason to smile,
Not everyone loves their neighbor,
And not everyone helps one another.
And just like that,
their innocence disappears.
Until then, they are to remain. In their bubble of joy.
Let them view the world in their own perspective,
As a bright and colorful painting.

Chicken Casserole
Mikaela Bartlett

She put the stars in my sky at night
And lifted my early sun
A skyline view, a red telephone
Words said few, thoughts yet roamed
Small bedroom and black counters
Warm afternoon and bright yellow flowers
A blueberry fridge and pale green walls
Sugar, a smidge, and plastic toy dolls
Her house was small, but it fit her soul
We sat together, eating chicken casserole

The Terrible Truth
Mikaela Bartlett

I can be the gun in the holster at your waist
Or I could even be the bait
You know I'd do anything for you
Tough break that you never follow through

I think your deception keeps the world turning around
So I'll bury the truth deep down in the ground
Six feet deep, so even I don't know
Clip the tag off your love that claims it faux

You're all smiles and false appreciation
Leaving me stuck in this hopeless damnation
At what point did you stop truly caring?
When did I stop truthfully sharing?

Everything I am, it's all usefulness
You would never know the definition of scrupulous
Must I explain everything to you?
No conclusions can you draw with your own tools?

I'll be a well-used dull-ended pencil
As for workers, I'm the most essential
Don't pay me a cent; I'll live off my spite
Just make sure your excuses are airtight

I've figured you out all on my own
Glass houses are hazards when you only own stones
I've got growing pains like the thorns of a rose
Rid yourself of me, my gods, and feel your wealth dispose

The Woman in White: A Sailors' Sea Shanty
Mikaela Bartlett

This past weekend I went a-walkin'
Down past the sunny shore side
Hummin' some old folk-song tune
But then, to my surprise,

My eyes beheld a beautiful thing
A stunning, staggering sight
For there along the sunny shore
Stood a woman in white

Her hair, swept over her shoulder
Had seaweed in its tangles
Not even the misty ocean view
Could ever hold a candle

She turned around and met my eye
And smiled a crooked smile
She was missing teeth, some top, some beneath
And her eyes went on for miles

She didn't move, and nor did I
I felt I would scare her off
She was nothing short of a drowned rat
And the thought of it made me scoff

This woman in white was no rodent to me
I would never have laid a trap
For rather I felt that she was the snare
And I, the helpless rat

Eventually she turned back 'round
And disappeared into the mist
Never again did I see the woman
Whom I'm unsure really exists

As she fell beneath the water
I then felt the blight
Fellow, turn around, if ever you come
Across the woman in white

Hellenistic Surrealism
Patrick Blalack

Canto Alpha

electric lutes   with waving phasers
delphic marble   strobed with lasers
ultraviolet   parthenon
with colonnades   glowing neon

olympian   glowstick torch
disco balls   adorn the porch
neon green   stone inscription
plato's cryptic   code encryption

crystallized   neon light
radiates   with kryptonite
disco dancers   run a marathon
a sonic rush   to heraclion

crowds line up   at cinema greece
for sophocles's   new release
the drama of   the unmasked persona
at panorama   shopping agora

futuristic   archaisms
mystify   the disco prisms
algorithms   can't compute
anomalies of   electric lute

olympus mount is   electrified
santorini is   mystified
it's so very   hellenistic
yet new wave techno   futuristic

Canto Beta

stoics hum   the synth bass droning
apollo's keyboards   zipping, blowing
muses dancing   to the drum machine
by aphrodite's   neon sheen

zeus's thund'rous gated snare
two digital harps the gemini share
electric lyres with overdrive fuzz
orpheus' moogs whoosh and buzz

homeric ballads with synthesizer
of alexander the hyptonizer
into the voice modulators
by sleek and icy contemplators

senseless sages with telegnosis
awakened with deep hypnosis
hippocrates' cure elixir prescription
and patmos island luau vacation

pegasus go-carts' accelerators
pythagoras' graphing calculators
cupid is getting quite platonic
and democritus less atomic

peloponnese is electrified
salamis is mystified
it's all very hellenistic
but never is it unrealistic

Canto Gamma

poseidon's fists moisturize
medusa's stares vaporize
sirens sing with fire truck drivers
archimedes turns mega screwdrivers

orion shoots a laser gun
at the astronaut icarus to the sun
hipparchus gazes telescopic
ptolomeus spins gyroscopic

athenians desired democracy
spartans desired oligarchy
but now just gyros filled with lamb
with tzatziki sauce ordered through hologram

gaia likes   geography
atlas likes   cartography
on the acropolis get   acrophobia
the djs jam in   hagia sophia

lyrics in new wave   symphony
mixed with mega   cacophony
racecar at noon   palindrome
demolition derby   in the hippodrome

hydra likes   electrolytes
aether likes   electrical lights
some are blind by   psychotic photons
and driven nuts by   neurotic neurons

korinthos is   electrified
zakinthos is   mystified
it's all very   hellenistic
still it's always   surrealistic

telos

No Childhood Home for a Renter
Erica Callahan

Dream easy, little child
Who returns home on break to her pink room
Painted walls, left unchanged
Marks on the lip of the wall; her height through the years
A chip in the door that brings her fond memories

Speak now, dear girl
Who returns to the house that she's lived in for three years
Walls left unchanged
No posters, no marks
No evidence of herself

How tall was I at 5 years old? How tall am I now?

Rules for tenants:
Rent due on the first
No paint. No holes. No markings.
Move within the year

Gulumf
Erica Callahan

I walk without aim
And I speak without purpose
I ask my thoughts to play a game with me
I think, for now, it will be fun

My thoughts run stray for hours
The day passes by and I have done nothing

I stare at the walls and I shudder
Not for myself
For something I can not grasp
It is a concept
Something inexplicable, unreal
I am inexplicable and unreal I think

I spend my life inside a world that does not exist
It does not belong to me
And I can not go home

Until Death—
Felix Campbell

Look at these picturesque lovers,
innocently kissing cheery cheeks,

prebubescently praised for their chemistry—
never mind they yet don't the know meaning—

who morphed into teens commanded
to marry, to be locked and chained,
to cherish each other for better or worse

like the roots of two trees mangled in mud,
squandering for nutrients or hoarding water,
choking osmosis until each leaf curls over,
every interweaved limb and fiber withering,

or like fungus leeching into paper skin,
ringworms staining virgin skin red, marked,

or parasites bloated from bad blood
like vampires sucking on veins until
their exsanguinated host crumples forsaken

into an immortal casket with their killer,
so even in death, they cannot part.

The Youth Pastor
Felix Campbell

those miracle mornings—
our sun-soaked secret dawns

of adventure—just us two—
setting off to save souls,

alone and trekking through
those holy campus grounds—

tin roofs glowing golden,
reaching towards Heaven—

and an office, a second home,
buzzing of stale florescent,

my bare feet kicking at
mold green garbled carpet—

not bored but lost amidst
swelling sweet pride in my

pastor father leading
lost kids—how could i know?—

bloodstained were the bookshelves,
sinful was the hand

holding my tender trust,
stuffed full of faith in my

pastor father paving
the way—how could i know?—

to Hell.

Eggs and Bacon
Felix Campbell

Sunlight pervades tight-lipped blinds
with brutal, unforgiving presence,
spewing heat into the throat,
an iridescent phlegm that clogs air
so only light lives in the lungs;
a thick beam burning brightly
which cannot be swallowed,
but must be kept on the tongue,
or spills down the chest to seize
command of slick muscles and pump
Daytime into these veins.

Temporal Confessions
Claudia Cooper

Close your eyes, lean back, relax.
Feel the gentle marking of my
felt-tip pen around your shaven cranium.
Cold, impersonal metal cuts in.
Feel the slow and warm flow
of your blood
down the contours of your face.
I pop your top off like the lid of my favorite jam.
Oh, it's just as gooey inside as my strawberry preserves!
In my instruments go, one-by-one.
Feel the pokes and prods in your gelatin world.
So easy to slice and scoop and shape.
Sometimes I get stuck—
Where do I examine next?
What will this fleshy mass reveal to me
once I can maneuver through the slime?
Aren't you scared I will take something from you?

I already did—
the moment you closed your eyes.
I took it.
It is much better off in my hands.
You won't even know it's gone
until you see it
in the hands of someone else.
For now, just relax and let me do
what I do best
what *you* trusted me to do.

Rod Wave
Daisy Calero Estrella

Are you ready to go?
My mind says yes
but my heart says no.
Too much history
Tainted with distorted truths
Contaminated with doubt
of what lies remain uncovered,
but it is all I know.
Pride says I do not deserve it
but maybe I do.
There is nobody else
I want
but you

cannot love me.
You are
an artist
erecting elaborate mosaics
freckled with illusions and false promises,
yet unable to hide the dirt
piecing your scheme together.
Next time,
Ask me.

How do I fool the one
who loves me?
Paint pretty portraits
until they no longer dry.
When they discover,
DENY
Insult
Ignore
Betray
Lie
Then, cry.
Beg
Plead
"Please *amor te amo.*"
Touch, then go.
Space
PRESSURE
Until the lonely forgives.

Buy her concert tickets
To see the ultimate
Heartbreak king.

You always loved him,
related,
but was it real or for convenience?

Fall back.
It was never serious
because
in the end

It's you
Always you
I hate you
I love you

Senescence
Chassidy Hearn

She
taking piece by piece
with certain instinct
The result was
perfection in a strange and startling way
Rhododendrons forming
The writing
beside the golden candlesticks
The room filled with
rhododendrons
How strange it was
so
languorous
This beautiful
woman
destroyed

she taking piece by piece with certain instinct the result was perfection in a strange and startling way rhododendrons forming the writing beside the golden candlesticks. The room was filled with them, even the rhododendrons obtrude how strange it was so languorous this beautiful woman destroyed

Will You Scratch My Back
Gwendalyn Henning

Friends since forever, I can't imagine little me without little you.
I escaped my family at your house and you escaped yours in my
company. We showered as friends, and we always held space for
each other.
So, will you scratch my back for me?
You left and we cried but we grew; you found friends more like you
and I found friends like me. My friends lied to me and left me out.
Will you scratch my back while I cry?
We grew and we tried and we failed and we came back together.
We live and laugh, lean and depend, watch old grainy movies
together.
Will you scratch my back tonight?
You start to change and lie and leave. I fight for you and those little girls.
Please scratch my back?
Just once more, scratch my back, break a nail, embed it in my skin
so that little girl will have something to scratch her back with.

For my Beloved
Benjamin Hernandez

My darling one
Let it be known throughout all the lands,
That you truly are the most graceful and elegant being under the sun.
For you were blessed with such purity and radiance when God crafted
you with his divine hands
Your hair is as smooth as the finest silk.
Your lips are the color of a cherry blossom.
Your skin is as creamy as buttermilk.
The love I feel for you truly is awesome.
I will love you when your silky hair turns gray.
I will love you when your lips lose their rosy shade.
I will love you when your skin wilts like flowers on a hot summer's day.
Your loveliness is eternal and shall never fade.
Nations and empires shall rise and fall,
And my love for you shall outlast them all.
Continents will change their shape and mountain ranges will become
a flat plain.
My love for you will remain.
When Gaberial sounds his horn to mark the end,
and the heavens open up, with you, in eternity I would love to spend.

The Shot
Mitchell Junious

Bullets blast to the brain
thrown like the blood stained
clothes that did not protect their
innocent families

Needles drive into the deltoid
short sickness to save yourself
still others choose natural
selection to sort the weak

Rockets riot to create rubble
ending and restarting
never-ending cycles to raise
status and reputation

Hamartian hope of the heart
a chance to try or better yet
to fail like every hero who
held the world in his hands

Destruction Devastation Death
Ready?
Don't worry
I'm recording

And I got the shot

Quiver
Mitchell Junious

We stand, a flight of feathers,
for our leper Leonidas.
Surrounded by Saladin's soldiers,
the demons of Damascus.
O Jerusalem, we defend
'till God delivers Montgisard,
or makes our feathers wings
to fly forever in glory.

But for now we wait.
Calm under heaven's skies.
For divine charge to fill our souls.
For Five Fold Crosses to fill the purse.
Clad with copper crosses upon our hearts.

Three whistles and we advance.
Two whistles and draw.
One whistle and the arrows whistle
in reply, penetrating the wind
and flying as feathers do
through the skies and over the fields
until they find their mark...
and we hear the silent crimson cries.

Declaring our victory.
With a single quiver.

Petrichor
Mitchell Junious

Seven score and seven years ago,
under the heat of the southern sun,
and the laws of Covington,
a farmer's martyrdom made sadness spread
from the firstborn to the seventh son,
in the land of antebellum.

On that day, the clouds came,
shielding the sky from the darkness to come.
Sown seeds ready for harvest,
wait while jealous neighbors,
soon to be invaders, plan to kill their kind
cultivator, leaving orphaned rows.

The first night they came,
but when they heard
the blast from his gun, all they could do
was turn back and run.

The second night, the same.
Not armed with a rifle, but
the gleam of his scythe
would ruin their would-be plight.

The third day they waited,
and the fourth, fifth, and sixth.
Each day the farmer's
defenses started to relax.

The seventh day came—
no sign of attack.
While the farmer slept, his
seventh son would be kidnapped.

The air grew heavy and humid.
Gray clouds began to grumble.
Winds abruptly twisted and turned.

With no help to be found,
in an altruistic flash, like the violent
lightning above, the farmer

made a pact with the
sky and traded himself to the men,
to save his son.

Tears rained down.
Sadness outpoured.
Crops withered in grief.
The children were left
vulnerable and defenseless.

Time went by. Rain stopped.
People forgot what happened
to the farmer on the now
drought stricken land.

Nearly a century and a half has
passed, since the farmer's self-sacrifice
saved his son. But peace cannot last
forever. New threats came to the
farmer's descendant's land.

At the first sign of unrest,
came a different kind of calm.
Petrichor filled the air to purge
all forms of distress and safety
from any possible scourge.

Timelines
Zoë Landers

April: We baked cinnamon cookies in
your dorm, and the drizzle of the rain left
heart-shaped droplets on your window.

May: We raced the moon home while
Taylor Swift's '*folklore*' blasted through
the speakers of your car.

June: We twirled in fields of highway
wild flowers, plucking petals singing
"*she loves me, she loves me not.*"

July: We packed up your things,
said our goodbyes, and the sweltering
sun hid our tears behind weeping sweat.

August: We talked on the phone daily,
and I watched the autumn leaves turn
the color of your hair.

September: You were too busy to talk,
but I wrote letters when I sat at our favorite
tree, and the birds practiced your laugh.

October: You didn't have time read my
letters, but you called when you could.

November: You didn't have time.

December:

January:

February:

March: I heard you changed your hair.
I bet it looks nice.

Sense me
Zoë Landers

Do not mourn for me when I am dead.
Know that even when the Earth
envelopes me, I appear

In the taste of the honeysuckle's
nectar, how it greeted your lips
as we picked flowers that
Spring morning

In the song of the cicadas, how
they hummed while we
swam in the lake that
Summer afternoon

In the sway of the reeds,
as they sifted with the wind
and we danced in the fields that
Autumn evening

In the smell of the rain, the
way it patted on the roof as
we sipped our chai in the library that
Winter night

In the brush of a stranger's hand,
how it felt almost like mine, but not
Quite.

Bedmaking
Zoë Landers
Eleanor Award for Undergraduate Poetry

Step 1. Lay your mattress pad across the bed,
Tuck each of the four corners tight.

> Cover the stains of your past,
> If you cannot see them, they do not exist.

Step 2. Wrap the fitted sheet around the mattress,
Careful not to pull too hard on one side.

> A fragile process to begin again,
> Too much pressure and it all unravels.

Step 3. Lay out the top sheet, even out the sides,
Smooth the wrinkles and creases, tuck the excess in.

> No one has to know what you went through.
> Glaze over the surface, cram the baggage underneath.

Step 4. Unfold the duvet, place it on the bed,
Tighten the bottom so it stays in place.

> Keep it together, you do not have the time.
> Bury the secrets so deeply they cannot escape.

Step 5. Fluff the pillows and place them in their cases.
Tweak the decorative throws till they sit just right.

> Use distractions to avoid questions,
> You cannot let them see your feathers poking through.

You've made your bed,

> Now lie in it.

Parasitoidism[1]
Zoë Landers

Weeping willow hair
Floats with the wind,

Bends of torsos
mimic grassy hills.

Freckles mirror constellations,
stretch marks clone ripples
from the lake.

Dried desert skin splits in a drought,
veins imitate purple lightning.

Irises swirl in Milkyway patterns,
rain trickles down
and pools
in cheekbone valleys.

Limbs extend from bodies;
fingerprints spiral as tree trunk
centers.

Intertwining roots strangle the earth,
draining it to keep us sustained.

[1]*Parasitoidism (noun): larva feeds upon the living host tissues in an orderly sequence such that the host is not killed until the larval development is complete.*

Girlhood
Zoë Landers

We paint pretty pink pictures,
and sing silly sappy songs.
We write whimsical stories about
the boys we want to last long.

We design dazzling dainty dresses
for our dreamy first-date dances,
We imagine our irresistible idols
as we read our ridiculous romances.

We collect colored crystals,
and form fairytale fictions.
We buy basic Starbucks
to feed our coffee addictions.

But we poise our perfect,
pretty sweet smiles so that when
'well-intentioned' weasels
wrestle their way in,

We can conform to their fantasies
and fetishes, and bury our
bodies beneath boys, whose
special 'suggestions' surely sour.

Matthew 15:8[1]
Zoë Landers

"To love her is a sin,"
You say, in between hits
of your blue raspberry vape.

Nicotine clouds burn your lungs,
and race to escape in foggy judgment.
But I breathe her in and her scent
ignites in me. I hold my breath to
savor each note in her perfume.

Last nights alcohol writhes behind
your eyes, you snooze your Sunday
service alarm. But I've memorized
the scriptures etched in her skin, each
sacred moment is heaven.

Hypocrisy wraps your tongue so
densely, Prayer's blade cannot pierce,
but I kneel before her, sing praises at
her altar, giving thanks at every
kiss down her spine.

"To love her is a sin,"
Yet, I confess, she is the
most divine being I worship.

[1] *"These people honor me with their lips, but their hearts are far from me."*

Mad Dog and Frog
Britton Larson

Mad Dog drags his muddy chain chasing Frog
Frog ain't too keen of canines
Ain't too keen at all
Mad Dog's mad tho
Says, 'Frog's leaping for a lick,

Sticking his nose in what ain't his"
Mad dog don't like Frog one bit

Frog don't mean no harm tho
He wouldn't hurt a fl—
Well, that's different

Anyways, Frog don't mean no harm to Mad Dog
See, Mad Dog scares away the Heron
The Heron's always pickin' on 'Ol Frog
Swooping into their swampy backyard

Mad Dog's always itching for a fight, on account of the Fleas

They really know how to get under his skin
So, Frog decided to help Mad Dog out
He hopped on over to Mad Dog's pen when the Heron swooped in
Said, "You Fleas should pick on someone your own size"
And he gave each one a lickin'

After that Mad Dog really weren't so mad after all

Now Dog scares the Heron
And Frog licks the Fleas
And they both live in their swampy backyard
Their story, bein' told by 'Ol Trees like me

Scrimmage
Britton Larson

Wide open, going long,
A leathery embrace, hands shaking with control, trembling.
I have you... You're here.

Don't drop it, Butterfingers

At a standstill, the wind ceased its sweet whispers cheering me on;
The cold settled in, pinching my ears pink. It's got my nose, Dad.
It's got my nose but I can't let go; I've got the ball and the cold can't
take it.

Come on back, you'll freeze out there

The world inhaled for a moment; the wind slapped me on the back.
The snow fell down into formation. I set to rush; they set to blitz.
An eagle's whistle cut through my chill, lacerated my fear, exposed
my heart.

You've got heart, just like your old man

Then I was rushing. I was hot blood on cold snow, a sure sign of life.
The ball was bound to my side like a bandage, covering a non-physical
wound.
The trees on the sideline waved me on; the weathercock pointed me
home.

That's my boy, run it on home

The welcoming porchlight hummed warmth into the air, his chair
was empty now,
A push from the wind made it rock reassuringly, the soft breeze
ruffled my hair.
The cold couldn't reach me under the porchlight's summer heat.

Wipe your shoes at the door, dinner's on the table

Love, a Loan
Chad Le

Love to me has always been away
Love to me was never here to stay

Alone is me
when I think love
Alone with me
when I think love.

Loan to me your heart and your soul
Because my own has been wrung and nulled
Its warmth and trust pay what was lost
The kindness and courage to overcome frost

Loan to me and I'll give you more
Because my life is bonded to yours

Only 2000s Kids Remember
Chloe Lopez

The squeak of the linoleum floor resounds,
Through the now empty gymnasium,
As the last third grader exits for their next class,
Just as the last one will,
In the final days of the building.

The demolition team will break down the walls,
Concrete colliding with stucco, linoleum, and brick,
Creating an amalgamation of browns, whites, and reds,
Until it cremates into a grey dust before it's dozed off,
To the local dump.

One day the light will turn off for the last time,
And the last graduating class,
Will dye their fading greys,
Moisturize their well-earned wrinkles,
And preserve themselves,
In photos on their daughters' walls.

Years before,
When the last of the teachers retire,
The faded plastic of the toys they once set out,
The yellowed pages gone soft from children's love
Of literature,
Will reside on the shelves,
Of descended family members,
Or on the tops of displays,
In a local thrift store.

"$3.99" reads the price tag,
On a set of *Captain Underpants* books,
With the inside covers labeled,
"If Found, Please Return to Miss Loyola,"
And then, "Room 202, Second and Third Grade Hall,"
And a partially worn front page,
As they sit,
Next to a once bright green plush,
of the infamous Magic School Bus character, Liz.

People on social media will share posts,
Of low quality and poor cropping,

"Only 2000s kids remember this,"
With a picture of DVDs,
A combination of Bill Nye,
Miss Frizzle, and Arthur.

And when those memories of the old school fade,
While the new school memories come into view,
This childhood memory of mine will fade away
To give way to my later years,
Innocence and bright saturation,
Slip through my fingers,
Into a faded stuffed animal figment,
Of Nostalgia.

Put It to Rest
Davonna Martin

I couldn't put it to rest then, so why would I put it to rest now?
A thought so infuriating, there isn't much you can do with it.
It's a thought I can never get over because
I work day and night trying to lose the memory that I wish I never
retrieved.
there's epiphany in my words when I say "I want to heal" or "I
want to forget"
I think back to the time when I had a mind that would only try to kill me
At one point, I was going to allow it that desire.

I have this crippling infatuation with my despair.
I'm just sitting in this pain that turns into anger.
and I rage and rage and rage with this thought that it will never get better.
and I know it won't.
Despite dwelling in my rage, I am just a little girl in a room
wishing, hoping, yearning
that I can put it to rest.

Reference Section
Raul Martin

Volumes:
You were not dirty.
You were not torn.
Your spines sturdy.
Your pages unworn.

Your obituary winks
at me in rosy, red ink:
discard.

Knowledge expired
like aired milk and bologna.
Knowledge reborn:
commodity.

Spinning Windmills
Raul Martin

The world needs giants.

Giants to cleft Don Quixote's contest
and spin windmills in Kansas.

Giants to spy on us deny being small
and help combat dark forces.

Giants to flunk our fit means of travel
and collapse wind into watts.

Giants to advise us when to munch
and when to judge our lot.

Giants to flout the world is burning
and help us put it out.

Maybe these giants are here.
Alive amongst people.
Call them spinning windmills.

Itemized
Raul Martin

The greeter reads the receipt at the exit.

2 MILK	007874235187 F	$3.06
EGGS 12CT	007874212707 F	$2.60
NESTLE WATER	000000009503 F	$6.98

The greeter thinks more paper pays for things.
Things do not know this.

The milk jug may learn as much
marooned on a barge
floating in the Gulf.
The Styrofoam egg carton bodes time
but in five centuries dissolves to grime.
Water bottles may discover this
had Apostles lamented and traced their ancestry
to bottling company: Nestle.

And yet, the patron culls the crumpled receipt:
tosses it because it felt strange in a pocket—
a clump of history mingled with lint.

Shackles
Kaelee E McCoy

Today was a rainy day.
I don't know where the sun went, I can't find it.
Everything is dark, and I can't find my way out.
I feel like Atlas holding up the world all alone, but I've yet to figure
out what crime I'm paying the price for.
My emotions are my bondage, and I don't think anyone will be
able to set me free.

Pillars of Light
Marquis Moore

i love the way my muse looks into my eyes.
irises of green stare into the softest parts of my soul.
i close my eyes as the outside wind blows,
and my breath hitches when his lips meet mine.

it's a foreign feeling of excitement.
the breath of new life.
from when your heart skips a beat to when your hearts meet,
you begin to think of two lives.

for you no longer love yourself but he who holds you close.
for the spirit of light is there to treat you right,
so, i fall in love with the feeling that's most enormous.

love is my muse.
it doesn't have a gender to its name.
it shines like the sun and reflects off a moon.
you can't escape it in the night and you damn sure can't escape it
in the day.

no matter how you look at it the picture is painted the same. it
looks different in different times, yet the picture is the same.

it's a pillar of light, he is.
it's a blanket of warmth, he is.
it's a feeling of excitement, he is.

love, he does it all.
he's the light that i see when i look at my mom's.
he's the light that i see when i give praise to my God
he's the love that i see when i'm filled with my pride.
he's the light that i see when i'm cumming deep inside.

he's my pillar of light.
he's my muse in disguise.
love is my life.

Stranger to Stranger
Grace Nicholson

Love, you,
You should hear the way I think.
I think you'd find solace in the way I think of you.
You are a gentle reader, guided by the tongue of another.
Another, who would gladly see you burn the world.
If the world were burning, I have thoughts I'd share with you.
I'd share with you the kindness unique to the human point of view.
The point of view focused on the way that we're so small.
We're so small that the burning world would engulf us all.
I'd engulf you in the gentlest of hugs, as a human being.
Being in such a way, that we are intertwined as the world burns.
We would burn as I burn for you, stranger.
Stranger, your soul burns hotter than the flames.
Flaming is my desire to share a gentler purpose with you.

You have something to say?
Say that you will be gentle as a human being.
That being human means that you are aware of our size.
That you would size us down from space travelers to infants.
Infants, who see through glossy lenses of love.
Lenses intrinsically designed for learning how to live.
Say that living small is better than burning the world,
the world, that we share as strangers who simply want to be heard.
Heard by those around us, who don't think us small at all.

I am small, yet I have something big to say.
I say that you are not without purpose or light.
Light shines through a window on a random day,
And on that random day you are seen as magnificent.
Magnificent and small and wonderful and there.
There you are. Are you not? Being bright and alive, stranger.
And stranger to stranger, if I saw me the way I saw you
I'd see myself as gentle and bold.
Boldly subduing the matches meant to burn.
Burning instead, the ideas planted inside by another.
Another, who has no love for you.
Love, I do.

T's and B's are a Tib Bricky
Grace Nicholson

swap your t's and b's

B stands for tig ol' Bexas Bibbies.
Understand, this is not in reference to
the ibby-tibby-bibby-commibbee and
Only concerns those with toulders on their chests.

The issue is this:
It's hobber than saban's tallsack,
Than Baylor Swifb, or even hobber than
Trad Pibb in his prime bime.
Seriously, its hob as shibb.

Bexas women suffer when their tubbs stick
to turning hob leather seats, which is tad enough,
but then it's coupled with swamp ass up to their bibbies.
It's enough to make teaubiful women bremble with rage.
Rage so tig it rivals the rage caused by Bexas toys.

Everything is tigger in Bexas, especially the sun.
The sun seems to seep every tib of moisture from
Our todies. Turning our skin and teating down from above
causing sweab to seep from our pibbs, tubbs, and toots.
Quickly, our todies tecome boxic wastelands.
You must be wondering why the women of Bexas stay
if their tooties are large, rotusb, and sweab so tadly
it causes them to tring extra clothes everywhere they go.
The answer is brubhfully simple:
it is merely due to pride, tragging rights and
of course, the earned appreciation for the winber's cold.

Bexas women with tig bibbs love the winber; they
Look forward to the branquil feeling of sweatless toots.
It is a small, yet wonderful respite that these teaubiful
Women long for during the long, hob Bexas summers.

Ripples
Christine Osborne

Fish clash in a crowded pond
stifling schools—can't breathe, can't
swim away from the squall.

Water freezing there, boiling here,
sunlight too gentle, now too harsh,
searching the pool for a safe space.

Forcibly ejected onto dry land,
gills gasping, fins flapping futilely,
pond vacated for bigger fish.

Swimming against the current
into a clear open spring,
a small fish in a big pond.

The old pond a distant memory,
a pebble's faint skip in the stream
with resounding ripples.

Cattail Marsh
Christine Osborne

God says good morning
with fingers of sunlight reaching, rays cutting the clouds
wispy tendrils of chill rapidly enveloped by daybreak.
Wide, flapping wings catch the breeze,
weaving to land in the wetlands with a quiet splash.
Squawking calls sing in cadence with the bullfrogs bellowing,
the cattails, paintbrushes nestled in towering fronds,
rustling in rhythm to the symphony's scene.
Bushy stalks sprouting toward heaven,
silhouetted against the amber canopy—
vees gliding through the honeyed horizon,
a final flight echoing into the evening as
God says good night.

Thy Dove sang a lullaby
Zachary Pruitt

To children dreaming on Your chest
By Thy mountain way on high

Water, earth, and sky
Must seem to be undressed
Where Thy Dove sang a lullaby

There is beauty in Thy
Grandeur to separate east and west
To look upon Thy mountain way on high

For here we shout crucify, crucify
Yet, even yet, no protest
For Thy Dove sang a lullaby

And by blood purify
And make in Thy a nest
To see Thy mountain way on high

In the promised by and by
Sons and daughters rest
For Thy Dove sang a lullaby
That we might view Thy mountain on high

Red
Zachary Pruitt

Was the sky
Filled with the call of death
Swirling, the ground wept
In tears that oozed
Every crack was filled
And every mountain fell flat
For the rivers ran like—
Red
Sweat and flesh
That boiled with love
Bubbling up like soda pop
And remains the scars
The gashes and bruises
that were made with—
Red
Eyes that held
The galaxy
Every moment
A touch from heaven
That seal with a kiss
The chains' removal
And from slave
To child
There has always been—
Red
Was never the end
But beginning anew
It was Life that could run
It could soar upon
The clouds
And make a home for
The orphan
And Life
To give
To have
And to never again be—
Red

Coma
Zachary Pruitt

what do i do... what should i do—

Emotions wilt as
I wail, and from Your heart
Seeds bring forth marigolds
To kiss my cheek.

what do i do... do You hear me—

Yet I succumb to the
Frozen pine,
The bite of winter air
Longing to feel Your warmth.

what do i do... please please—

The Sparrow tells me
My soul is greater than the dove,
But the thorns that scar
Beg to differ.

what do i do... oh God—

I wish to be with You
Where the grass flows sweet,
To never have to worry
If I'll fade with the dead.

what do i do... help me please—

Not My Will
Zachary Pruitt

You know a tale of iron and bone,
and what of man and pain,
of struggle and hate,
of teeth and tattle,
when one becomes
greater than the least
and forfeits his soul—
You know a tale of wood and spirit,
and what of woman and thirst,
of hatred and courage,
of truth and misery,
when another becomes
more than mindless worship
to taste freedom with one's heart—
You know a tale of stone and fear,
tuned with fire and doubt,
like a harp of forgetful medleys,
yet the hands cared
and the eye mended the herds
to heal the bountiful sorrow
there to partake the wreckage of body—
You know a tale of life and faith,
tuned by the drought of belief,
like a melody of unrest,
but with ears to capture
and an arm to wholly praise
let us wander in solemn grace
and die in unrelenting friendship—

our final goodbye
Abigail Serrano

when we say our final goodbye
i will be saying goodbye
to my oldest bad habit

i will be saying goodbye
to a love that never existed
a love i
wished
hoped
and begged for

when we say our final goodbye
i will miss you
i will miss the comfort
we gave to one another

but when we say our final goodbye
i will say goodbye
to a version of you
that i never got to see

and that will be the greatest comfort

tell me you love me
Abigail Serrano

tell me you love me
just once
let me hear those sweet words
escape from your lips

tell me you love me
like narcissus
loved his own reflection

tell me you love me
and my heart will be yours
my body will be yours
my mind will be yours
and my soul will be yours

tell me you love me
even if it's a lie
my body will continue
to be yours

tell me you love me
because i love you

When I was... BRO-KEN...
Darlene Thomas-Pierre

When I was... BRO-KEN... broken in two
one side, all of
me—one side, half of you
you hurt me badly—still
didn't wanna hurt you

When I was... BRO-KEN... all broken down
kept a brave
face—broken down to the ground

When I was... BRO-KEN... broken for real
kept moving
forward—kept my half of the deal

When I was... BRO-KEN... broken in heart
didn't know how to
end it—didn't know where to start

When I was... BRO-KEN... broken and numb
feeling all stupid—
feeling all dumb

When I was... BRO-KEN... broken, hurt and confused
feeling mistreated—
feeling misused and abused

When I was... BRO-KEN... broken in time
this moment
no reason, that moment no rhyme

When I was... BRO-KEN... broken in mind
life all off
kilter—everything out of line

When I was... BRO-KEN... broken and scattered
heart all in
pieces—spirit all shattered

When I was... BRO-KEN... soul filled with strife
although you

BROKE me—I still claimed my life

When I was... BRO-KEN... I hoped it'd get better

                                                    this thing

               seemed over—couldn't be deader

When I was... BRO-KEN... lost and then found

                                                       I lost

            me, I found me—feet still firm on the ground

When I was... BRO-KEN... God still knew my name

                                                not gonna

          let you change me—still me, still the same

                                refusing to crumble—not

      gonna crash

                   though my whole life is burning, my

            heart burnt to ash

When I was... BRO-KEN... something in me died

                                                  I know

            I'll be whole again—strong, true and tried

When I was... BRO-KEN... broken in two

                                                     one

           side, all of me—one side, none of you

BRO-KEN   HEALED   WHOLE

A Giant in My Eyes
Darlene Thomas-Pierre

For my Daddy

When I was a little girl,
and my pigtails flew behind me when I ran…
I thought my dad stood 9' tall,
If anybody could (I thought) I know my daddy can.

He was a giant in my eyes

He was big and strong, with arms like Popeye…
I thought my dad could defeat any enemy
And fight any battle…
He could fix anything and do anything

He was a giant in my mind

Now I'm all grown up
And I know now that he quietly taught us
His values and ethics by the way he lived
And how hard he worked…

We're all a little older now,
we don't run around with our pigtails flying,
my daddy isn't 9' tall,
and now that I stand eye to weary eye with him,

He's STILL a GIANT in my eyes.

A giant not in stature, but in character
A giant not in *the* world, but in *my* world

Even when he's gone, to me he'll always be standing strong,
this man who did not compromise, will always be a giant in my
eyes.

teach me how to free me
Darlene Thomas-Pierre

Educate me, don't berate me, if you want to teach me to be free.
Teach me to write, but teach me to spell first, so I can write correctly.

Go on and entertain me, but then go ahead and train me in the art
of how to "be" me.

If you want to feed me, lead me to the freed me, lead me out of
utter poverty so I can feed you, them and me.

If I'm wrong chide me, if life is looking, don't try to hide me; lead
me to the bona fide me.

Tell me what's the deal, show me what is real, tell me how you
really feel about me.

Don't spare the rod and spoil me, tell me about God and then ap-
pall me. Be careful and think about what you call me.

When you whip me, don't abuse me. When you correct me, don't
confuse me. So, they'll know you really raised me.

Give me the keys to unlock my psyche, when they physically jail
my body. Help me rise above the mire when I'm the economical-
ly-trapped-in-my-environ me.

Help me to find the center "me" when my spirit is in bondage to
the street. Advise me how to be a whole me when they try to take a
part of the soul "me."

Teach me how to know me when they tell me what I can't be.
Teach me how to see me when they try to force invisibility on me.

Teach me how to free me, so I can be the best me I can be. Teach
me. Free me. Free me

Always think of the power words have. (There's life and death in
the power of the tongue —Proverbs 18:21.) Because everything you
hear and read will affect your actions! Therefore: ALWAYS be...
POSITIVE! *And above all: Be DEAF when people tell YOU
that you cannot fulfill your dreams! Always think: God and I can
do this!*

Here I stand, flat-footed and sure, unrepentant and strong!

Helix King
Keely Viator

Coiled by the shallow light of dusk
That catches glinting teeth,
White like snail shells in gravel,
Curls a figure crouching
Over a man pressed to the pavement,
The spirals of knuckles engraved
On his face as milky tears
Salt the tar road underneath.
Impenitent, its ferrofluid form combs
The silty night as it rises,
Fist seeping mucous blood
Across the pavement,
Marking its escape route with the ease
Of something that knows
It may take its time leaving,
Hook its tail on street lights as it goes.
It wipes out the fruitless
In self-defense, in brutality,
Under the claim to have fun
And the repressed desire
To circle back around and feel the twist
Of its own foot on concrete.

Wolf of Hands
Keely Viator

Playing coy at first,
It tames
With lazy taps
On the shoulder
Before, frenzied
By the smell of trust,
It gnaws off its fur,
Leaving only a pelt
Of ligaments twining—
digging into one another,
The insatiable immortal
Tunneling through body
      For feeding.

It cannot tell ego from prey.
It pinches
Elbows, tugs shirt hems
Into flea-bitten dens
Where it can palm mouth,
Suffocate neurons
Until there is no space
For dreaming.

Snapping at necks,
It disobeys
All boundaries
But expects guests
Will raise paws
When it commands
      For shaking.

Overgrown
Jeri Wolfe

I built a barrier out of serrated and tangled vines
and you taught me how to let someone prune the knots out.
Mother nature gave you the mind of a savant—
we are all born from this wild garden of natural knowledge,
but you have grown from the softest dirt.
I expect to be plucked with a calloused and firm grip,
as I am an unweeded flowerbed left overgrown;
but I watch your patient hands sift through the foliage
to find the bright orange tulips that would make the reddest rose blush.
I am as predictable as blue violets,
while you surprise a crowd with sun-kissed marigolds.
You have shown me beauty in a thorny stem,
the fangs a protection against prying claws;
you pick me from the bush with caution,
gently avoiding the pricks and letting the bloom open its petals.

The Cycle of Growing
Teri Wolfe

I watch the grass grow taller
as it tries to race me in height,
but alas,
a week passes, and the Sunday grass
is cut, releasing
the dewy aroma into the air.

I, too, get mowed down and
admired until I'm too tall,
until I need to be trimmed down.
I can hear the lawn mower's
engine roaring, blades whirring
to humble me. But not now.

Today, I'm towering above the blades.

The dirt pays no mind
to our endless battle to the top.
It stays the same:
the old rocks and pebbles,
the minerals and grime
sit in their permanent spots,
unlike me and the grass
in our fleeting state of being.
The dirt is perfectly content
staying aged and unfazed.

The grass and I,
we are too absorbed in the way
that the mower's wheels drive
over us, clipping and trimming
just a few inches off—not a lot,
but enough to keep us going.
I wonder if the grass
mirrors my exhaustion
from this never-ending cycle
of growing.

Today, I'm calling a truce.

I stand in the forest of grass,
interlacing my fingers with
the blunt-cut green blades.
I will stay for a while.
Today, I'm keeping the grass company
and the dirt will hold us both.

Poetry in Translation

The Widest Road*
Translated by Jo Youngeun
Oliphant Award for Poetry in Translation

Sometimes in life
The way to go may be invisible
Don't get frustrated, take your time

The road doesn't disappear
for being covered with snow,
The road doesen't disappear
for being buried in darkness

Just hold your broom
Sweep away the snow
As the dawn breaks
The road will appear

The widest road
Is always inside of me

*Translated from Korean in Yang Kwang-Mo's *Does the Flower Suffer in the Shade* (2023). See next page for original version.

가장 넓은길

살다 보면
길이 보이지 않을 때가 있다.
원망하지 말고 기다려라

눈에 덮였다고
길이 없어진 것이 아니요,
어둠에 묻혔다고
길이 사라진 것도 아니다

묵묵히 빗자루를 들고
눈을 치우다 보면
새벽과 함께
길이 나타날 것이다

가장 넓은 길은
언제나 내 마음속에 있다

Translator's Note

Poet Yang Kwang-mo's poem "The Widest Road" was selected as the handwriting verification phrase for the Korean college entrance exam in November 2023. This phrase, chosen by the Korea Institute for Curriculum and Evaluation, is drawn from the works of domestic authors containing content that can convey positive hope and encouragement to the examinees. Typically emphasizing the beauty of the Korean language, these phrases range from 12 to 19 characters and must include consonants for handwriting identification.

Poet Yang Kwang-mo, during his journey of overcoming numerous failures and despair, discovered his dream of becoming a poet while drafting a bucket list around the age of twenty. Since then, he began writing poems to comfort those immersed in despair and sorrow. "The Widest Road," a product of such a period, encapsulates the profound insight that a road does not disappear simply because it's unseen. The poem conveys the message that as long as one does not lose the path in their heart, the road always exists.

I perceive college as more than a mere educational institution; it's a sandbox, an experimental space before stepping into society. Moments of failure might bring sadness or despair, and sometimes it takes considerable time and effort to emerge from these valleys of sorrow. However, persistently facing various failures within this sandbox, I believe, will eventually lead us to hear the voice from deep within our hearts.

From this perspective, I hope that all members of the university community—students, faculty, and staff, regardless of age, gender, race, nationality, and other social backgrounds—can freely experience failure in this 'experimental space' and find their own 'Widest Road.' With this in mind, I undertook the translation of this poem.

Creative Prose

My Dear Sister, Marie
Erica Callahan

Reports about my sister Marie's death come in waves from local news stations. Her story is being covered by shabby reporters who only care about the chance to gain a little publicity. Her life is being observed under a magnifying glass and stripped of all humanity. She's no longer a person. She's immortalized in the form of poorly written articles as the girl who drowned. It's something she would've hated.

She's nothing but the 6 o'clock news.

I grow restless hearing about her. I hear her name echoed in the hallways at school. Time seems to freeze now that she's gone. No one can think about anything else but her. The name Marie makes me tremble.

Marie Marie Marie.

I am not myself anymore. I am the girl with a dead sister. People whisper when they see me, and I become surrounded by a constant stream of ushered voices. She haunts me like a ghost. I feel as if she never left.

Marie was the standard for our family; something I could never dream of reaching. She was always the pretty one, her hair a lovely gold and her eyes sky blue. I looked bland next to her. She was smarter than me too, and when she died, the family seemed to believe that any hope of success died with her.

Marie cast a shadow onto me both in life and death. She held onto the title "golden child" with an iron fist. I desperately wanted to get just an ounce of the adoration and praise that she was constantly on the receiving end of.

I hated that Marie died. Not because I lost my sister—because the loss of my sister sealed my fate. I could never beat the competition I didn't have. I could never prove myself better than she was when she was dead.

I hated Marie. Both alive and dead.

However, I feigned sadness. If I let people know that I was indifferent to her death, it'd make them suspicious. The last thing I wanted to do was get that kind of attention. So I played it up.

They needed to see that I was heartbroken. I knew that if I held out for long enough, my apathetic attitude towards the situation would be acceptable. Perhaps then, people would move on. Maybe then, I could get some recognition.

But of course, that was only wishful thinking.

Marie had become a state qualifier for our school's track team mere days before she drowned. Everyone knew that if she didn't turn out to be the scientist who cured cancer, then she'd surely be an Olympic gold medalist. Success was written into her blood.

I wasn't impressed. I was irritated by her constant need to prove her worth. Why was it so important for her to constantly go above and beyond? It was something that I just couldn't wrap my head around. It was as if she existed purely to outdo me; to be something that I could never be. What an awful way to live.

Now, it doesn't matter. It didn't matter what Marie did while she was alive because she wasn't anymore. The world would keep going on without her stupid mathlete brain and her incredible stamina. Someone else would win a gold medal and someone else would find the cure to cancer. These things did not die with Marie.

However, I died with Marie that day. There's something peculiar about the way people cope with loss. Some choose to ignore it, some choose to seek counseling. However, a few become deluded and seek out the dead in everything.

My mom said Marie was in the sunset when the sky smeared itself with beautiful colors. She said Marie spoke to her through the wind and kissed her with the rain. Every passing thing that my mom saw art within was Marie.

To everyone else, I held some semblance of my sister. I get comments about my eyes being like hers, how we have the same nose, and how we have the same flushness to our cheeks. I became one with my dead sister.

Mom never made those comments. In fact, I think I caught her flinching at one of them. I didn't understand at first, was I not beautiful enough to be Marie? I had to teach myself not to mind this.

My mom also died with Marie. She floats around the house now like a ghost. She's so still and quiet that I barely notice her at all. She sits and stares at nothing for hours at a time. Her fingers trace the spots where Marie used to be. I don't mind her and she doesn't mind me.

One night, she puts a plate of food in front of me at the table and it's the first real dinner we've had in a while. I say thank you. I tell her I love her. She says nothing back.

She won't even look at me.

My mother's been on medication for her depression since she was a teenager. She stopped taking it shortly after her death. I think in some way she feels like she deserves to feel bad. She would feel guilty letting herself move forward, so she purposely makes herself miserable. She's pathetic.

I grow bitter towards her.

In the months following Marie's death, my mother became unrecognizable to me. I had no choice but to leave her behind. *I* could move on. I was *going to* move on. I stopped caring how messy the house got and how my mom and dad barely spoke anymore. I stopped caring that food stopped appearing on the table. I stopped caring about anything that pertained to Marie.

I had my first date a week after I stopped caring. My first real date with a real boy. He's from a different school district. He doesn't know that I have a dead sister. He won't ever see Marie's nose on me. He will never see her in the sunset.

When I turn 15 I don't bother to spend the day with my family. They'll only talk about how I'm now the same age as *her*. I hang out with my boyfriend. He got me a bracelet. It's a pretty little thing that's slightly too big for my wrist. I marvel at it.

I spend every day with him. He doesn't care that I'm perpetually quiet and sometimes get lost in my head. He doesn't care that I sometimes float around just like my mother. He walks with me wherever I wander aimlessly. He sits and waits for me to come back when I stare into the void. He's apprehensive towards me. We don't talk about much at all. Sometimes he flinches when I turn too fast.

We last five months before he finds out. The moment he utters her name I fall instantly out of love with him.

"You didn't tell me you had a sister," he says to me. He brushes my hair out of my face. The gesture makes me feel warm.

"It doesn't matter," I tell him.

"A dead sister is pretty important, Elizabeth." He never calls me Elizabeth. He's supposed to call me Lizzie. I stare at him. Not in shock. Not with any particular emotion at all. I stare at him like he's a stranger and let out a little sigh.

"Alright," I fold. I throw my hands up in defeat. "My sister's dead. Big deal." His mouth gapes.

"Big deal? What the hell is wrong with you, dude." He's surprised that I don't care. He's shaking and looking at me as if I'm some sort of monster. It doesn't matter anymore.

We ended things that night. It's the first real pain I've felt in awhile.

I begin to fall behind in classes, but that's okay because I'm grieving. My teachers offer me extra help like a good person would. Everyone looks at me like I'm a mangy stray dog. They only feel pity. They will never feel pride towards me.

I feel myself slipping.

Summer is a dark cloud that looms in the horizon as the semester comes to a close. I know summer will be particularly hard for my family. Marie was born June 16th. Summer was her time of year. She had countless pretty pink bathing suits and she tanned with perfection. She was the poster child for the season.

I finished up the school year, passing where I didn't deserve and leaving with way fewer friends than I started with. No one wants a friend that they constantly feel sorry for. Likewise, I don't need friends who walk on eggshells around me. I hate the looks everyone gives me when I walk out those doors. They fear they'll lose me. I think they should know better.

My ex-boyfriend sticks around. He tries to make amends with me. He wants me to talk to a therapist. He thinks I'm hurt way more than I think by my sister's tragic and sudden passing. I appreciate his concern and care for me, so I let him make his theories. I let him pretend that he's helping me.

We argue frequently. He tells me that I don't make an effort to get better. I get close to spilling the truth to him on several occasions. That I don't care at all what happened to Marie. That Marie isn't important anymore. I am real, Marie is not. It's a truth that people can't seem to understand.

Why can't they understand? How can I get them to see me? Why do they still only see Marie? He's never even met her and yet he cares more about her than he cares about me. I'm forever a victim of her regime. I will never escape her.

Not at this rate.

It becomes clear to me what I must do.

If I want to remove Marie's dead weight, I am going to have to remove proof of her existence in relation to me. I must become a girl who never had a sister. I have to detach her completely from myself. I've learned that outrunning Marie is harder than I initially thought. I've already done so much. I can't stop my efforts now.

Can I tell you a secret?

This is not a recount of my past struggles, this is a confession.

I am talking to you.

Marie's death was ruled as an accident. She happened to be wearing a pretty pink dress the day she died. One that sparkled in the light and made her skin glow. She looked perfect the day she died. She always looked beautiful. She always wore pink.

It was said that she fell in and the weight of the dress dragged her down. They say that she bruised herself in the fall. She must've thrusted around on the rocky bottom enough to leave wounds. The peaceful, unsuspecting pond she drowned in held the perfect cover up.

Are you ready for my secret?

I killed Marie.

I knew that as long as she lived, I never could. I knew that if I didn't get rid of her before she truly had the chance to succeed, I would never accomplish anything worthwhile. Marie and I could not exist at the same time. One of us had to go.

Of course, I didn't consider the consequences of my actions. Marie was much stronger than me. Had anyone cared to check, they would've found the evidence of her struggles. Her nails, always done up to perfection, had pierced my forearms. Her grip had bruised my wrists. I had the upper ground for once. I pushed her in. She couldn't pull herself up this time.

You promise not to tell, won't you? There's not much more to go. I'm almost done talking.

I cut contact with my ex-boyfriend despite the fact that I think that I truly love him. After he learned about Marie, it was too late for him. He fell in love with the idea of what I could be if I allowed myself to heal from it all. He, too, loves the marks Marie left on me. I can't stand to look at him.

I grow to resent everyone who says her name. I grow to resent myself for letting her continue to drag me down. I understand that if I'm ever to escape, I'm going to have to get away.

So I ran. I leave my old life behind and allow myself to lay my roots down in a new place. I take up a new identity. I give up Elizabeth Williams and become Mary Ann Davis.

Like Marie, I become a story on the 6 o'clock news. I see the number of missing posters grow slimmer the longer I walk on.

Mary Ann Davis kills only once more. She kills the me of the past. I do not mourn that girl in the same way I do not mourn her sister. I grow apart from anything that could've saved me.

I know I will die in the little, soulless town that I've made my home. I will die cold and alone.

But I will die knowing that I *did* change the lives of many people. I ruined the life that Marie could've had and I ruined everything for the family that loved her. I created a haunting memory in the minds of everyone who once sat beside her. I changed the world for the worst.

I have ruined everything.

It's the most magnificent thing I've ever done.

Check Mate
Felix Campbell

Carmine stood in the shadows, not knowing if it was appropriate to let them know he was there. It wasn't that he had been *trying* to hide from them or anything. It just sort of happened. But then he'd gotten curious about what they were up to—curiosity is a natural thing, so you can't really blame him, right? Besides, anyone would be intrigued if they had gone for a spontaneous walk in the woods behind the neighborhood and found their two best friends sitting in the moss, talking in low voices. It was mysterious as hell!

But now he had been standing here watching them for a few minutes, and he didn't want them to think he'd followed them, or that he was spying on them! But he wasn't quite sure how to make it seem *natural* that he'd come across them. Which it was.

Maybe, he thought, *they don't have to know I was here. What they don't know won't kill them. And maybe...maybe it's alright to listen in on them. They are my friends after all. Friends tell each other everything.* And so, he decided to stay there in the shadows and eavesdrop on the two for a little while. Though, it wasn't really eavesdropping—they were friends! And if he walked over to them right now, they would probably tell him anyway. So, no harm no foul.

As Carmine tuned into the conversation, Tomas was hissing something like, "...freaks me out, Isa! He started acting like this last year, and it's only gotten worse since high school. I know you've seen it, too! Right?"

Isabel plucked a piece of bark off a nearby tree and ran her fingers over the smooth backside of it. A few pieces of her ebony hair fell into her face, but she didn't bother to brush it away. "I don't like to talk about it. I told you that."

Tomas rolled his eyes. "I know, I know." He paused to poke at the moss, and a deep scowl took over his still boyish face. "But we can't just *ignore* it. That's how bad things happen."

"I don't know," Isabel mumbled. She sniffed the bark, like she couldn't think of anything else to do. Maybe she didn't want to be there. Maybe it was Tomas's idea. Tomas did that sometimes—he had a habit of ignoring his friends' opinions because he assumed they wanted to do everything he wanted to.

"You don't know *what*? I've told you everything—"

She cut him off by tossing the bark onto the mess of curls atop his head. "Not that, dummy. Trust me, you talk about it all the time. I only meant," she corrected, "that I don't know if it's a good idea to. Talk about it, that is."

Tomas only stared at her as he took the wood out of his hair, clearly not understanding.

Isabel's gaze danced through the clearing and the shadows among the trees. Carmine held his breath when her eyes wandered over to his hiding place (though he wasn't hiding, of course), but she didn't seem to notice him.

She lowered her voice. "I have a feeling it's better if he doesn't find out we know."

"Well—" Tomas waved a hand dismissively, "I just think he ought'ta be sent away or something. He clearly needs some help."

Carmine scowled. Was someone bothering his friends? He didn't like that. No, no, no. He didn't like that one bit! He didn't like it when people messed with Tomas. He despised it when people messed with Isabel. *Who is it, Isabel? Just tell me.*

Isabel shook her head at Tomas. She plucked a little flower from the ground and spun its stem between her thumb and index finger. "Maybe he's ill."

"Maybe he's a—"

"Don't be mean, Tomas!" Isabel snapped. In her outburst, she had bent the poor flower's stem, leaving it crooked and pathetic. When she noticed this, her flashing eyes glossed over with this indescribable kind of sorrow. "Oh! Look what you made me do! Now it's dead! Dead and ugly!"

His thick brows furrowed in confusion, and he let out a snort. "Don't be ridiculous, Isa. Flowers die once you pick them, you know. You're the one who killed it, not me."

Isabel turned away from him and sniffled. She set the flower down gently on the moss. Carmine thought he could see a tear glistening in her lashes. Maybe he imagined it. Or maybe it was just the sun glistening on her cheek. Or maybe it was just because that's what Isabel did: she always shimmered like she was the sun itself.

"Don't you think we ought'ta mention it to someone, at least? Maybe we could tell our parents. Well, *your* parents. My parents said I was just being jealous. I told them, 'Jealous of what?!' *Him*? No way!" Tomas crossed his arms and stuck his chin into the air.

"Why do we have to tell? He isn't hurting anyone…"

"Not yet!"

"Tomas," Isabel warned, her eyes growing dark. "He's sweet, and you know that. He cares about you. Maybe you *are* just being jealous."

He balked at her, jaw agape. Then he collected himself and scoffed. "Why can't you see it, Isa?! I'm just trying to keep you safe! Because *I* care about *you*."

Isabel tossed her hair over her shoulder and sat up tall. She pulled her knees to her chest and hugged them tightly. "Maybe I don't need you to keep me safe," she grumbled into the denim of her jeans.

Tomas groaned and flopped back into the moss. "You can be so difficult sometimes."

"It goes both ways, you know."

He grunted in response. For a moment, he lifted his hands into the air above him, like he might start to talk and gesture wildly, but then he just let his arms fall to the ground beside him. "You have to admit he's weird, at least," he said softly.

Isabel shrugged. "I think we're all a little weird, don't you? That's how it is."

From his cover behind a wide oak tree, Carmine's lips pulled into a grimace. Isabel was too kind. If someone really was bothering his friends, then it didn't matter whether he was weird or not. This perpetrator had to know he couldn't mess with them. *Just tell me who it is, Isabel!*

Tomas sat up suddenly, a panicked look in his eyes. He grabbed Isabel's shoulders firmly, shaking her slightly. "You don't *like* him, do you, Isa?!"

Isabel's eyes widened. "Oh, Carmine? No, no—not like that! He's our best friend. We made a deal, remember? Back in elementary school? We promised we would never date each other when we were older."

Carmine struggled to withhold a gasp of indignation. *Have they been talking about me all this time? Tomas wants* me *to be sent away?* He clenched a fist at his side, trying to hold down the anger rising in him.

Isabel grew silent for a moment and began picking at a flannel patch in her jeans. Tomas let go of her and sagged in relief. He pressed his palms into the moss behind him and leaned his weight against his arms. He had this smug grin on his face.

"I take promises seriously," Isabel whispered after a little while of silence.

Tomas shrugged. "We were just kids, Isa. Don't take it too seriously. But," he sighed, "I'm glad you don't like him. That would make things...weird."

"Because we're all friends."

"Because *he's* weird," Tomas corrected. "I don't like you spending so much time with him. Even if he is our friend." He said the last word as if it tasted sour on his tongue.

Carmine's blood boiled. *How dare he! He's always wanted Isabel all for himself! I should have known!* He was preparing to step into the clearing, to confront that son of a—

"And I don't like spending so much time with you, Tomas! You're being immature and mean!" She let go of her knees and pushed herself off the ground. "I don't know why you two fight each other so much these days! I liked it better when we were all friends!" She dusted herself off as Tomas rose to stand beside her. He reached for her arm, but she slapped it away.

"Isabel!" He pleaded.

"No!" She stuck her nose in the air and stamped her foot. Crossing her arms, she stepped away from him. "I'm done talking now, Tomas—you should be talking to Carmine, instead. And until you two figure out whatever is going on between you, I'm not going to hang out with either of you. So, you can let me know when you're ready to be friends again, like we *used* to be."

With that, Isabel turned on her heel and stalked out of the clearing (thankfully in a different direction than that which Carmine had come from). Soon, the sound of her receding footsteps was lost to the woods, and only Carmine and Tomas remained.

With Isabel gone, Carmine yet again wondered if he should reveal himself. *Isabel did say that she wouldn't hang out with me unless Tomas* and *me are...agreeable.* Though, he wasn't sure if it was possible. Ever since they had started their freshman year of high school, things had gotten progressively worse between them. They wanted different things from life, but they wanted the same girl. And poor Isabel...

Carmine made his decision.

Taking a deep breath, he stepped around the tree and into the clearing. At first, Tomas didn't seem to notice him, but then a twig broke beneath his foot, and his friend's attention snapped to him at once.

"What the hell?!" Tomas gasped, his brows scrunching to-gether. He took a step back and took up a defensive position, his body tense. "How long have you been standing there, you creep? Do you just follow Isa around everywhere now?!"

"I went for a walk and here you were."

Tomas scoffed. "Likely story."

Carmine shrugged, shaking his head. "I can't make you believe me. It's up to you."

"You're pathetic, you know that?"

"Says the one who's using underhanded techniques to woo his crush," Carmine retorted. "I mean, seriously? Fear tactics? Trying to make her *afraid* of me? You must be intimidated."

"*Tch.* Please." Tomas rolled his eyes. "You don't intimidate me, Carmine. And I wasn't trying to manipulate her, you dick. I was *concerned* for her. You've been acting...off lately. Don't deny it."

Carmine blinked slowly. "Have I?" *Maybe a little moody, but...*

"Yes!" Tomas exclaimed, throwing his hands into the air. "You have this look in your eyes these days. Sometimes you look more like a crazed animal than a human, much less my friend. What has gotten into you? Are you on something?"

"Oh, bravo!" Carmine snorted. Then, he serenaded Tomas with an obnoxiously loud round of applause. "You're hallucinating! Maybe *you're* on something."

"Don't play dumb with me—I know what I've seen!"

"You only see what you *want* to see!" he snarled. "It's been that way since middle school, Tomas! You've been trying to turn everyone against me ever since you started crushing on Isabel! And now?! Now you're trying to frame me as some kind of...some kind of *lunatic*?! You only want to keep Isabel to yourself, and you don't care who you have to take down in the process, do you?!"

"Oh, that's real rich coming from you!" Tomas snapped back, anger flashing in his eyes. He took a menacing step toward him, his hands clenched at his sides. "Don't try to play the victim here! I know what you did earlier this year! I know you were saying shit to Isa, lying to her! Telling her that I was secretly dating that girl from our Home Ec class last year! You're just afraid that Isa's gonna choose me—you know she will! And that's why you're being so fucking weird these days!"

He pointed a finger in Carmine's face, a gloating smile on his lips. "Just give up."

Carmine crossed his arms and put all his weight on his left leg. He was taller than Tomas, and he used that now to his advantage, staring down his nose at him. "I'm not giving up on Isabel. And hey, if you don't want me to assume you're dating chicks, then maybe you shouldn't kiss them."

Tomas's jaw dropped. "I did *not* kiss her!"

"Oh, really? So, it was just some other kid with curly brown hair wearing the basketball team's sweats?"

"Even if I did kiss her—which I *didn't*—then it wouldn't have meant anything! You shouldn't jump to conclusions like that! And you shouldn't go behind my back and spread rumors when you don't even know if they're true or not!"

"Maybe it wasn't me."

"Maybe you're an *idiot* if you think I'm gonna believe that shit," Tomas hissed.

"Okay, basketball boy."

"What the hell is that supposed to mean, *chess* team captain?!"

"Exactly. At least I have a brain." He tapped the side of his head twice, grinning.

"Yeah, well maybe I'll have to fix that!" Tomas shouted, stepping closer. A bit of spit flew from his lips, landing on Carmine's sleeve.

Carmine wiped the spit away with a calm expression. "Are you threatening me, Tomas?" he asked, raising a brow. He clicked his tongue disapprovingly and shook his head. "That's a bit drastic, don't you think? And you say *I'm* the crazy one."

Tomas's nostrils flared as he tried to calm himself down. "Is this all just a game to you?! I swear you don't even care about Isabel! You just want to win!"

Carmine pressed his index finger into Tomas's chest and smirked. "You say that as if you aren't playing, too."

Tomas grabbed his finger and sharply pushed it away, not caring if it hurt him. "Because I'm *not*," he said in a low voice. "And you shouldn't be, either."

Carmine sighed and stepped back. "You say you aren't playing, yet you're trying to take me down, as if I'm your opponent." His face grew serious, and he leveled him with a stern glare. "Do whatever you think you must to get your girl, but I know how this ends, Tomas. And I never lose."

He smiled at his friend, who was staring at him in horror. He didn't like it when Tomas looked at him like that, like he was some kind of villain. But this was all necessary.

He glanced back up to see his friend sputtering for a response, clearly at a loss for words. Carmine smiled. Then, having nothing left to say, he gave him a small wave and turned away. He left the clearing with Tomas still standing there dumbfounded, and he followed the same path Isabel had used earlier.

That's right, that's right. I never lose.

The Odessey of Jane McMarah
Daniela Contreras

It was my first night away from my parents, my family, and my home since I was born. I took a moment to let that settle in, stopped my bike before the corner's stop sign, and took one more look at the two-story house in front of me. I saw the brick texture brightly lit by Christmas decorations and shadowed by the huge inflatable characters. I saw the warmly lit windows, but specifically the one that was always turned off. It had a dried-up succulent with long dried stems that made up the image of bygone good glory days. The pot was purple, which the darkness did not reveal, but it was my sister's signature color. I stared until my eyes felt hot and my cheeks flushed, which gave me a sick feeling at the exposure to the cold thin air. My whole body thudded with a heavy heartbeat, and the wide breaths were cold and burning. Then, I felt a hot rush that pounded all the way to my head as remembered I that it was less than an hour till twelve, and I had to hurry if I wanted to make it there by the end of the night.

My older sister, Pearl, taught me how to ride my bike, which used to be hers. It was a faded purple with rusted dots and scraped paint. There were about three pieces of white sparkling strips left and mud stains that did not seem like they would ever come off. I was gifted a bike for my birthday that same year, but I rode hers nonetheless. Holding on the handlebars felt like holding her hand. Pearl did not need a bike anymore after getting her 2014 red Sedan. Because of the rules, I would have to ride in her backseat unless it was nighttime. Then she would let me slip into the passenger seat as she sped through the neighborhood all the way to the outsides of McKinley Airport. We sat on the grass on the other side of the wired-out fences, away from the building and at the sight of the planes.

"Imma be on that second row tomorrow," she said in their last ride, "on tha window seat. And, I'll wave at yuh, so yuh better be lookin'."

"There's no way I can see that fah Pearl!" I whined to her, and her smile faded a bit.

"Heur, come with me."

We walked to her car parked on the side of the road. She dug into her trunk which was partially packed for the next day and pulled out a camo cap and placed it in my hand.

"Yuh better take care of this, okay?" She said, choking on a laugh that held a hint of sadness. "It's tha only backup I have."

"I'm not so sure, Pearl, wontchu need it?"

"I'll just pick it up next time 'round if I need it, how 'bout that?"

"Won't that be too long?"

She placed the cap on my head.

"Private McMarah!" She said placing the cap on my head. "Let's enjoy tonite, okay?"

"But really, Pearl, what 'bout our New Years, huh?" I said looking nervously at the cluttered trunk.

I think Pearl noticed that because she closed it and walked me to our usual sitting spot below a willow tree.

"Look," she looked me in the eyes with a caring sternness. "I'm not sure how New Years will look like. This is temporary yuh know? But, Janey, I don't wanna sugarcoat yuh that life will continue changin'."

I just stared at her.

"But hey, come heur."

We walked to the tree and she pulled out a small pocket knife.

J

P

She carved.

"This is *the* spot for the Odesseyes of Pearl and Jane McMarah, and now it always will."

There were no cars on the street. Everyone seemed to be indoors with lighted-up windows in the neighborhood. The houses were lined up with similar front lawns and mailboxes at the edges, with numbers on the same side. Even the sequenced Christmas lights seemed to have a pattern: mostly white but with some color-ful houses in between. They all bought their decorations in one of our few stores, so all the blown-up characters seemed to be from the same show. Wide-grinning snowmen pointing the way home with their candy canes. Reindeers with sparkling eyes and shiny bells carrying jolly, rosy-cheeked, waving Santa Clauses. Mrs. Clauses standing near entrances holding a plate-full of smiling gingerbread mean cookies. I felt like a moth drawn to a flame, mesmerized espe-cially at the windows that had no curtains where warmth radiated from smiles and hugs and the pure presence of all the guests.

Two red lights flashed in front of me. *Shoot!* Someone saw me. It was Mrs. Trey's 2016 Toyota Sienna, and that meant trouble. We faced each other, but instead, I saw Mr. Trey in front of me, driving his wife's car. I instantly felt relieved; Mr. Trey is a private man, so he won't tell my parents. His face seemed puzzled, but he stretched out his hand for me to keep riding. I could think of no greeting and Mr. Trey did not seem to ask for one, so we both kept going to our paths.

I wondered what he could be going for with most of the places closed down, and I hoped that he would make it back soon. I also wondered why he did not stop to speak, a few months ago he would have asked.

"Hey, Pearl...little Janey! How're we doin'?"

"Nothin' yuh need to worry 'bout Mr. Trey!" Pearl would respond.

I kept pedaling until I reached Mrs. Wilson's house. She was a recent widow whose children all had gone off to bigger universities and then bigger jobs in bigger cities so that she only had her porch lit up for company. The small woman sat in a rocking chair.

"What are yuh doin' in the cold, honey?" she said in an insisting tone, with no other purpose than to hear a fellow voice, "Yuh'll miss tha fireworks."

I made up my mind that I'd stay, but not for long. I got closer to her; I couldn't let her start the year alone. Pearl would spend hours talking to her and Mr. Wilson. She was the one who walked next to her at the funeral; the children who came stood in a monotone, motionless line.

"Oh, Pearl, darlin' it's yuh!" She always confused my name with my sister's. "Now how is yuh sister? Did she come home?"

She seemed to read the answer from my face.

"Well, now, I know she's thinkin' 'bout yuh too," she responded. "Yeah, she's thinkin' bout yuh, so it don't matter where yuh are because yuh're together somewhere, somehow." She looked up to the sky as if she were talking about Mr. Wilson and her children.

I heard people making their way to doors and kids running with packets of lighters and sparklers while their parents carried bigger packets of fireworks. I had to go or I'd be late.

"I'm sorry, Mrs. Wilson. I gotta go, but Happy New Years!" I said followed by a quick hug.

"Okay, now, Happy New Years!"

I pedaled, tired, to the ends of the neighborhood when the fireworks started going off. I started to cry *Too late! Too late! Too late!* I kept repeating in my head. I could see them in a distance and I could hear them around me while on the empty highway. The sound faded to a minimum by the time I reached the side of the grass. I felt a hot rush and, in a movement, sat down on the grass, next to our willow tree. I ran my fingers through the P and saw how close it was to J. Every year, Pearl and I would make it a game to look at each other when the clock struck. I took off her cap and sobbed, holding it close to my chest; hopeless at the year ahead, the year that had begun so bitterly alone.

"This is the spot for the Odesseyes of Pearl and Jane McMarah, and now it always will."

I'm sorry.

I pedaled back defeated, still holding the cap in my hands. I was tired and drained. I had no energy to think about the people who looked for me because I had failed to look for Pearl. Mrs. Wilson stood on her porch as she saw me ride by.

"Pearl! Darlin'!"

"No!" I exclaimed and she seemed to jump back. "She didn' come!"

"Well, now, did yuh forget already?" she responded holding my face up. Without much force, she took the cap and placed it again on my head. "Yuh're together, somehow, somewhere."

I looked up to the stars with Mrs. Wilson. I wondered if Pearl had picked up that gesture from Mrs. Wilson, and we somehow stared at each other in some way.

I tried to picture a P and J among the stars.

"Always, Pearl."

The Morning Hope Returned
Daniela Contreras

Friday, 8:32 p.m.

Esperanza's cat died when she was six, but she did not cry about it until she was eight. Her older sisters were all crying in the living room that morning, especially Teresa who had discovered the body. It was probably the first time she had heard "dead" and heard it so many times in a day. But she didn't shed a tear until her 8th Thanksgiving when a lady she discovered was her aunt came over and asked about the cat she had given her sister five years ago, and her mom responded that he had died. Her bedtime was at 9 o'clock and it was 9:28 when she could not hold herself any longer and sat up on her bed and wept deeply. It took her about a week to mentally bury her cat, but the sadness never quite left. She never told anyone out of shame. And she felt guilty to have allowed herself to feel so much because now just about anything would lower her spirits. But no one needed to know. After all, she was Esperanza, a first-generation graduate in a high-paying job. Esperanza, with her own apartment in the big city. And so, Esperanza reached for her melatonin pill bottle and aspirin that drowned out her aching active mind for the night. She took out the small circles and lined the bottles back in their order of use, starting: B-12, B-6, D-3, Iron Supplements, Aspirin, and Melatonin. She tilted her head upwards and swallowed the small circles pushing her head back. She rocked her head forward at the view of a window showing a starless, light-blue night sky. Then, she headed to bed, although the thought of her cat felt a little stronger than before.

Friday, 9:33 p.m.

It takes 10-15 minutes to fall asleep and she felt it had been longer than that; however, she did not check if that time had lapsed because the radiation from screentime messes with sleep. It is recommended that screens are avoided at least 30 minutes before. She gave herself a chance to drift off as she tried to not move and breathe deeper; she would soon go to sleep like that. It was a Friday night; she could spare a few minutes longer to fall asleep. She thought about how people don't usually sleep with a bedtime on Fridays and how she always did. She did not like to stay up, even on weekends because her mind stopped working mechanically and started losing itself in thought. Her days were simple and pragmatic: work and errands and every so often going out with her work friends. That usually gave her a headache. Looking at screens all day tired her eyes. Grocery stores were too bright and noisy. People outside the office behaved differently, and she did not know how to react to that or join in on more than a casual conversation. But she did wonder if she was missed; they did have a house party today. She barely missed her cat and he was dead, how much more could she be missed?

Friday, 10:45 p.m.

She checked the time, she felt it had been too long to not be able to fall asleep. She stopped force-shutting her eyes which was causing her a headache by now. The party was probably still going on or just about wrapping up. They probably were not surprised that she did not show up if they had even noticed. The first times she said no to the parties she got texts, but no one really contacted her anymore; it had been too long. It took her cat dying for her to consider him.

Saturday, 12:23 a.m.

It might have been her phone screen that was keeping her awake now, but it had been too long for that. Her eyes were so adjusted to the dark now and she had given up in keeping them closed to try to sleep. So, she stared at the empty walls, the textured roof, and the starless city night. She had no family pictures; she never took the time to print them out and buy frames. She wondered if her family had pictures of her, but could she expect what she did not give? She thought of calling them. She had only called her family on special occasions, so they would question why she called and why at this time. She did not want to explain why she never did. It's not that she did not care. But she didn't take the time and at some point, they caught on to that and stopped calling too. She missed them tonight, after so long, and that made her feel too guilty to call. She wondered how long it took her family to forget her cat. How long had they grieved a dead thing?

Saturday, 2:14 a.m.

"You have reached the voice mailbox of Teresa Cruz, at the end of the tone, please record your message."

"The number you called has a voicemail box that has not been set up, yet…"

The party had to be over by now, but maybe everyone was asleep. Maybe they had erased her contact. Maybe they knew how insincere her call was, how she called only because she could not go to sleep. And what could she say? It wasn't to catch up or a 'just because.' And it was not to talk about her dead cat. It dawned on her how strange of a creature she was. She only cared for that cat after she knew it was not coming back. It was until something was gone that she cared. Her friends were gone, her family was away from her, and her cat was dead. Maybe it was disappearing that made a presence for her. But, she had disappeared; and that made no presence for anyone who once cared. She thought about how long it would take for someone to notice if she was actually gone. Her family would not notice until the Tuesday before Thanksgiving when she would not call to ask what she would bring. But maybe they would think it was the next step of detachment, and it would be until that dinner that they would see something was wrong. The people she called would call or text her back, but she did not think it would mean too much for her not to answer. It would not be until Monday that she would be gone for them, and maybe it would take a day or two to figure out that it was strange for her not to have shown up yet. But, would they try to figure out why she was gone? Maybe she had finally taken a vacation, even a new job. No one knew her deeply enough. It would be when delayed rent built up and her boss would want to fire her for all the days she had missed at that point. All the isolation she built would make it take so long for anyone to notice she was gone. It took her two years to know her cat was gone. She could be gone at any second. She could rest her mind, and no one would hurt.

It had a taste of freedom.

Saturday, 4:37 a.m.

She had lived a healthy life. She woke up at 5 a.m. and took vitamins B-6 and B-12 for energy. At lunchtime, she took D-3 and Iron supplements. At 8:30 she took an aspirin and melatonin to rest. Then, she went to bed at 9 p.m. She played by the rules that built her lone empire of success. But it had tumbled down, and she stared at the floor, hugging her knees. Yellow stains and saliva trails were connected to washed-out yellow pills and a trail of small ovals and circles scattered on the white carpet. She felt completely lost, unable to move or act or know what to do from here on. But she waited to start her day again, her alarm would ring soon.

Saturday, 5:00 a.m.

"You have reached the Suicide and Crisis Lifeline, if you think this is a medical emergency, please hang up and call 911. A representative will be with you shortly."

She wasn't gone yet; she had not disappeared. She looked out the window; there was a string of orange starting to slowly come up.

"Hello, thank you for calling. This is Rosario with the Suicide and Crisis Lifeline, could I get a name from you?"

She saw how the sun was coming up.

"Esperanza."

El Vals
Daniela Contreras

Imelda saw all her new life in neatly piled boxes. She looked proudly at the stacks like a cardboard empire almost too good to take down. The week before she had driven to the small studio with building tools and furniture boxes filling in white spaces with a wood color desk, table, bookshelf, cabinet, bedframe, and a nightstand that would be her home altar. Now, she scanned through the towers for the *Cleaning Supplies* labeled box she left at best disposition and sawed off the tape with her new home key. Once she started on the other boxes, it took her longer than effective time to get things in their place because she had to make up a place, her own order. She waltzed around from place to place, from one part of her small collection of furniture to the next. She did feel silly thinking about how much excitement could come from putting up her own collection of cutleries, but it was a small reminder of how far she'd come to have her own cutlery set.

She popped open her *Shelf FRAGILE* labeled box and started stocking the racks of her shelf with a small book collection, a couple of yearbooks, albums, and picture frames. She picked up a particular clear box with rounded corners. She looked through the fragmented image of a golden crown surrounding its smaller replica. She walked to her sink and ritualistically uncovered the lid. Imelda crowned herself once again and fixed two front strands of hair into makeshift curls like the day she became "a woman" according to Quinceañera tradition. She waltzed "El Vals," or what she could remember of it. And Imelda again danced again from one side of the bridge of childhood to the next: womanhood. The piece in her mind done; she looked down at the box and carefully ran her fingers around the small crown for her "last doll," which in her case as in most cases with quinceañeras, became the last time she got gifted a doll. She returned to her workstation and searched for the pink, flower-patterned shoe box where she'd packed the porcelain doll. But, no matter how far she bent down, or how many things she scooted out of her way, there was no shoe box. She moved to her clothes, but only found white or brown shoe boxes. She doubted that she would misplace her doll with her Cross and Saint figures, yet she searched with no result. She searched through the rest of the boxes: kitchenware, bed dressings, and office supplies, and then returned to the ones she already searched. She took down her towers, one by one, but there was no shoe box. It took her about three rounds of the same boxes, and her almost empty house now had no clear spot on the floor. Imelda dug through the pile of jackets and cups for her car keys and headed to her car, hoping she had just left her behind.

The empty car built on the rush. She was hot despite the cold wind, despite her jacket being in left her studio. She rushed back in and rushed out with the keys for the rented U-Haul that was still latched on her car. With her phone flashlight, she walked in, moving it from side to side. She walked carefully, her gut in the ground. There was only gray metal reflecting each small step. She hit the right corner again, but there was a dull reflection; she came closer.

Imelda looked down at her fallen soldier, at the bent-in, wrinkled, pink, flower-patterned cardboard box. She ran her fingers through the box before picking it up. Now she felt the wind. She picked the shoe box up and held it close to her as she, slowly now, locked everything back up and trudged back to her studio. It was no use trying to remember why she had piled the box in the U-Haul instead of her car or why she had not packed it in *Shelf FRAGILE* box to begin with. It already took all the hurt in her heart to carry the broken box that she couldn't give much response to those pangs of regret. She placed the box on her kitchen table and opened it. Picking up the doll, shattered bits of rosy cheeks, caramel skin, and brown eyes fell along with her right leg and most of her fingers. She shook off the dust and slowly took the mutilated thing to her bathroom sink. Taking the hand towel, she cleaned up the red ruffles, chipped arms, dancing shoe, and remains of a once-soft face. She crowned her again and fixed the two front strands into makeshift curls before taking her in her arms and waltzing her the way she was supposed to say goodbye to girlhood as tradition held it so. Imelda took off her own crown first and then placed both back in the clear box. She took her doll back to the shoe box and straightened it before closing the lid. In the corner of the top rack of her closet, Imelda laid to rest the small thing and placed the crowns on top. She returned to her shelf and continued stocking it up.

To Leave or to Stay
Claudia Cooper

The road leading to the multi-story complex was long and isolated from the rest of the city, the whole property having been closed off with a chain-link fence with barbed wire facing inwards. The security at the gate had been friendly enough—as friendly as those kinds of people get—with their fake smiles and squinted eyes. Darcie didn't let it get to her though; she had been waiting for this moment for half of her life. Citadel, LLC was the leading innovative technology company in the country with several branches scattered about, but this was the headquarters in front of her. The real deal, where everyone else wanted to be, including Darcie since she had seen the ads playing between episodes of her favorite cartoon. This concrete and colored glass monstrosity towering over her and her tiny car was the same as in the commercials, a hub of genius and risk-taking.

Parking her car and grabbing her suitcases, Darcie's eyes barely left Citadel headquarters. There was a growing sense of tension within her body as she walked closer: excitement or nerves? She couldn't tell, but regardless of how she felt, she was already here. She had already signed the work contract, signed the lease, and moved half-way across the country to start her dream job as soon as she had left college. Darcie couldn't believe her luck, not when her own colleagues had also applied and been rejected or offered positions at other branches.

The entrance housed more security guards, who looked over her shiny new badge before scanning her from head to toe. She was given clearance after answering a few questions that were just "standard protocol, ma'am." Inside strangely felt the same as the outside: clean, manicured, and carefully curated. Even the people, despite how crowded it was, moved in an orderly fashion with strangely quiet footsteps and passing murmurs of conversation. Darcie didn't know whether to be amazed or creeped out. Ignoring the streams of quiet people, she followed the directions on the map on her phone to the dormitories.

Ten minutes and one U-turn later, Darcie made it to the entrance of the dorm, which was tucked into an inconspicuous corner of the lounge. On her way, she had garnered a bit of attention, accompanied by friendly smiles and curious looks, but none had stopped her to talk. Darcie wasn't bothered by it; she rather disliked having to exchange small talk with strangers. Inside the deceptively large dormitory, several narrow hallways cut into the brightly painted walls of the common area. This is where Darcie had concluded with finality that she was lost. The hallways were unmarked, so finding her room was a matter of stumbling upon it. Unless she asked around, of course.

Darcie gathered her nerves before approaching a thin woman sitting on the couch and enjoying what looked like tea. "Um...hello," Darcie greeted with a little wave of her hand. "I'm Darcie Lincoln, and I'm new around here. I was wondering if you could help me find my room."

The woman looked up from her cup with a small, polite smile. "Of course," the woman replied before accepting the paper handed to her by Darcie. The woman's brown eyes briefly scanned the information before widening at something. "Oh, we seem to be next-door neighbors! I'll show you the way."

The woman stood up, still holding onto her tea cup as she led the way, going down the middle hallway on the far-left wall. Darcie quickly followed, her suitcase slightly hindering her mobility as the fluffy carpet created quite a bit of traction. "Thank you," Darcie breathed with a sigh of relief.

"It's no problem," The woman replied cheerfully, waving her hand as if batting away Darcie's gratitude like a pesky fly. "That's just what we do around here. We help each other out—no questions asked. I'm Alyssia Cojak, by the way, and like I said, your next-door neighbor, so don't hesitate to come knocking at my door for any questions or to simply hang out. I'm always looking for new friends."

"Okay, cool. I'll keep that in mind."

Darcie was relieved she had seemed to make a new friend so soon and quite easily as well. That was one less thing she had to worry about being in a new environment. The first thing Darcie did when she found her room was log into the company app, checking her newly acquired task list. Her first day was tomorrow, but there was an orientation for new hires that was mandatory to attend. Darcie looked at the scheduled times before deciding that the one starting in twenty minutes was the one she would go to.

As a way to distract from the anxiety starting to build, Darcie studied the map of the headquarters, charting her path to the exhibition hall where the orientation was to take place. Being early was better than being late, so Darcie set off fifteen minutes before the start of orientation. It only took eight minutes to get there, the exhibition hall already packed with people. Darcie was surprised by the number of attendees; surely, they weren't all new hires. It wasn't until she grabbed a pamphlet and leafed through it that she discovered the founder of Citadel was to be making an appearance.

Darcie had a feeling that the whole company showed up just to catch a glimpse of the elusive genius billionaire. With this new information, Darcie's nerves morphed into pure excitement. The quiet chatter near her was loud enough to catch what was being discussed. Charles Smith, the big boss, was really gracing them with his presence—might even say a few words of encouragement. Darcie could hear the unadulterated admiration lacing the workers' tone. She couldn't fault them for she idolized the man as well. Charles Smith was the reason she became a programmer. His contributions to the field of AI and robotics were revolutionary, spurring a whole generation of youth to follow in his footsteps.

The orientation seemed to drag on as she waited for Charles Smith to make his appearance. Fifty minutes later and parting sentiments booming over the speakers, Darcie felt bitter and lied to. Then, a thought crossed her mind: Charles Smith is a busy man. He didn't have time to attend every orientation. She had just chosen the wrong one. Plus, there was always next time. This was the Citadel headquarters after all—the boss lived here along with everyone else.

Darcie made her way out of the exhibition hall, noticing she was one of a very few who did. Even though the next orientation time was in two hours, the workers stayed and continued with their quiet yet excited murmurings. A chilling thought bubbled to the surface: how long have they been waiting in there?

Back in her room, Darcie began to unpack her things. She finally took the time to truly take in her surroundings. The room was pretty standard in size, with just enough space to comfortably maneuver between closet, bed, dresser, and desk. The walls were light grey and floor the same cream-colored fluffy carpet of the dorm hallways. It was bland but cozy, with a little square window for a bit of sunlight to peek through over the desk. Without it, Darcie was sure it would feel like staying in a hotel—boxed-in, impersonal, and temporary.

Darcie hadn't been here that long, but a feeling of missing home suddenly washed over her. There really wasn't much to miss: a little old town with a declining population. Darcie could remember the day she first heard Charles Smith's voice in Citadel's commercial. A charismatic quality with a musical cadence entranced her young mind, her constant ramblings of robot maids and AI reaching singularity entertaining her parents for years. Darcie couldn't go back home, not when she promised her parents that she'd make something that would change the world—just like Charles. Darcie released a sigh, deciding that she should just get some sleep. That is if she could even manage with the nerves of her first day tomorrow.

The next day arrived and Darcie found herself in an office with four other occupied desks inside. The clacking of keyboards and scribbling notes filled the space. Darcie wasn't sure what to expect, but it felt exceptionally normal. Nothing like the "innovating" or "risk-taking" she'd thought she'd be doing. Darcie figured she'd have to work her way up to that—getting hands on with programming robots. For now, it was writing strings of seemingly useless code, grunt work. It wasn't until break time that anything interesting happened.

Darcie gathered around the watercooler along with her officemates, barely listening. That is until Charles Smith came up in the conversation—something she was starting to suspect happened frequently around here. The workers were discussing the frequency of Charles' public appearances, both inside and outside the headquarters. Very rarely did he leave his laboratory located on the restricted upper floors. Darcie also learned he kept a tight circle of staff around him—those people seemed to actually be doing the "big boy" stuff. It was a coveted position obviously, and Darcie wanted to prove herself worthy.

With renewed passion, Darcie worked efficiently at her job before returning to her room. On her way, she encountered Alyssia. The extroverted woman followed her back to the dorms, trying to convince Darcie to attend the daily social activities hosted by the company. "Everyone goes, it's a bonding experience!" Her neighbor tried again.

Darcie wasn't one for social situations that involved larges masses of strangers, so she declined politely with the excuse of being overwhelmed and tired from her first day. A week passed just like that, with Darcie working hard, her coworkers fixating on Charles Smith and Citadel as if hobbies and pop culture didn't exist, and her declining Alyssia's invitations to the company's social events. Today, however, before Alyssia left, Darcie asked about a couple of things that had been on her mind. "Everyone really seems to admire Mr. Smith around here...I mean, I do, too but...they talk about him *constantly*. How come?"

"Well, he's a great man, is he not? He's the founder of this company, the guy who created everything in front of you. I mean, *c'mon*, his AI manages this place," Alyssia began to ramble. Darcie began to tune out before focusing back in when Alyssia mentioned his vision for Citadel. "His goal of a common unity is why going to the company social events is highly encouraged. We're a unit here, a family if you will. And Charles Smith is the father."

Something didn't sit right with Darcie upon hearing those words, but she couldn't quite pinpoint why. This company was run differently to others, that's what made Citadel headquarters so special. Yet doubt seemed to creep in. Darcie asked another question. "What even goes on at these social events?"

Alyssia seemed to brighten up at the interest Darcie was showing. "Well, it's different every day. Sometimes it's singing, sometimes it's dancing...sometimes it's just chatting over snacks. Today we're having a concert. One of the guys performing, Jay, I work with him in the customer service department, he's pretty good at the drums. It'll be a lot of fun, and it might help energize you!"

Darcie thought it over for a moment before finally agreeing. She really hadn't been enjoying her time here, drowning herself in work before sleeping it off. She was having a hard time relating to her coworkers, so maybe attending one of these little social events will turn things around. "Alright, I'll go."

The concert was held in the same place as orientation. The overhead lights were turned off, leaving purple and pink strobe lights to dance within the moving crowd. This was a stark contrast to the quiet atmosphere of the workplace; the people seemed to be finally letting loose in the most hedonistic way. Darcie watched as waiters walked around with silver platters, small paper patches saturated in what she was sure was hallucinogenic drugs going from tray to mouth. Darcie declined when the waiter offered, but Alyssia accepted with a wide smile.

"It's part of the experience, you know. It heightens our reception to those around us," the woman giggled before beginning to dance to the music like the others around them. Darcie's heart sank to her stomach. "This is what you've been missing out on!"

Darcie wasn't dancing, and she certainly wasn't having fun. She wasn't even sure she wanted to be here, not just at the concert, but the very company itself. This is definitely not what Darcie signed up for. Something was very wrong with this place, and Darcie should've seen the signs sooner. Just as she was about to leave, screams began to erupt within the crowd.

"It's him! It's him!"

"It's Charles Smith!"

Darcie stopped, eyes moving towards the stage as a middle-aged man walked into the spotlight. Even from the back of the room, thanks to the numerous television screens hanging around, she could clearly see his face and expression. He looked charming and benevolent.

"My beloved employees, I hope you have not missed me too much." Charles Smith's homely, crooked grin was met with the crowd's cheers. "It's been a while since I've attended one of these things, but it seems like everyone has got on just fine." Shouts of agreement rang throughout the room. "I come with the purpose of announcing the new selection of a team member after Terence, rest his soul, has passed from one of our experiments. Innovation comes with unexpected dangers, but I know my employees here at Citadel headquarters are up to the task." Another round of cheers and applause. "Applications for promotion will be available tomorrow afternoon. Have a good rest of your evening."

With that, Charles walked backstage and was gone. Darcie was stunned at the brief appearance of her elusive boss, but she was more so shocked to learn of the death of a Citadel worker; the blatant disregard for human life was appalling as she watched people continue to dance and talk excitedly about the possible promotion. It was like Charles hadn't mentioned Terence at all. How common was such an occurrence here? There was no outside news of deaths, or even injuries at Citadel before; had similar instances been covered up?

"Isn't that great, Darcie?" Alyssia asked, wrapping an arm around Darcie's shoulder, a smile stretching across her face. Darcie didn't dignify the question with a response. Something was very wrong with this place, these people.

Darcie realized in that moment her dream had been a waste, a lie. She would never get that promotion, and even if she did, she could die and no one would care. No one that she truly cared about—her parents and friends outside the headquarters—would know she was gone. Struck with regret, Darcie recalled that she hadn't spoken to her parents since she left. It hadn't even occurred to her, caught up in everything that Citadel presented, that she hadn't left the headquarters or gone outside. It seemed such a hassle with all the protocols one had to go through. Besides, the headquarters was generous in providing amenities.

Darcie wanted to leave, get out of this place before it swept her away and swallowed her whole. Yet a frightening thought butt its ugly head into the forefront of her mind: she couldn't leave. Not after signing her work contract, not after her promise to her parents to change the world. Darcie didn't want to go back to her little hometown, yet what exactly did she have here? Where could she go from here?

Darcie felt trapped, maybe just like everyone else here. Maybe that's why they go to these stupid social events to get high. A distraction from the fact that this place was a glorified prison cell. Charles Smith and Citadel, LLC was her dream goal, but it was an illusion. Charles Smith is just running a cult, and Darcie can't do anything about it.

The Cycle of Man
Morgan Irvine

It's been raining for three fucking days straight. Isaac couldn't stand it anymore. He was starting to go crazy being cooped up inside all the time, especially inside this place his dad was trying to call a home. Isaac knew it was never going to feel like a home, even after months of being here, he still couldn't find a reason to love it.

He didn't want to move into this place, especially not somewhere it seemed to rain more than anything else. He also didn't want to move for plenty of other reasons. He didn't want to leave his friends, his childhood home, and he definitely didn't want to move just so his dad could follow some chick across the country.

His dad had a bad habit of finding a woman and moving fast, like, really fast. For the most part, Isaac could handle it. It usually resulted in the woman moving in for a period, his dad would do something to upset her, mostly in the form of cheating, and she would move out. The cycle would then continue with the next woman. Yet, this time things were different, or that's how his dad put it. They were the ones being relocated. His dad claimed it was for a better job opportunity and that this woman was the real deal. Isaac wasn't an idiot, but he could pretend to be one. He had been doing it for eighteen years.

Every year there would be at least one woman who would be the "real deal." His dad would sit Isaac down and tell him that he was ready to settle down and that he was done playing games. He would start to cry and tell Isaac that he wanted to give him a real mom. Then every year Isaac would sit there and rub his dad's back as he cried and tell him that he was proud and that he was thankful to his dad for wanting to give him a mom. His dad would then dry up his tears in seconds, hug Isaac, and go back to his office. Isaac had the routine down pretty well.

He didn't mind not having a "real" mom. He did have one, when he was a child, but she passed before he could form any real memories. Sure, he had pictures, but for the most part she was just a ghost of someone he was supposed to know. Some days, like today, he resented her, but he knew it wasn't her fault. He just wishes she was here to control his dad. Maybe he wasn't always like this, but Isaac would never know.

Isaac sighed as he pushed the thought out of his mind and made his way to the kitchen. He was starving and his dad's new girlfriend, Marissa, seemed to always be cooking or baking which was a bonus at least. His dad rarely cooked, so Isaac always counted his blessings when he did date someone who could.

As he walked across the hall his ears perked up at the hushed voice of Marissa, whispering intensely to someone. Isaac walked into the kitchen, curious as to who she was talking to. As he came into Marissa's sight, he watched as she quickly hissed a "bye" to someone before shoving her phone in her pocket and turning fully to Isaac.

"Hi, hon. You hungry? Dinner is almost ready, and I was just about to whip up some brownies for dessert. Your dad should be home in a bit." She laughed nervously as she bent down to search the cabinets for a pan.

Isaac wondered who was on the phone. It was probably his dad, and from the way she hung up, she did not seem happy with him. Not surprising at all.

"Oh yeah, that sounds great. Was that him on the phone?"

Marissa stilled for a split second before continuing to rummage through the cabinet. Finally she found the pan she was searching for and pulled herself up, placing it on the counter. "Oh no, it was my coworker down at the office. She doesn't know how to do anything on her own," She dramatically emphasized "anything" and began pulling the ingredients she needed from around the kitchen. "She feels the need to call me over every simple thing." She let out another stiff laugh.

Isaac nodded, "Oh yeah..." he trailed off, not sure what else to say to this woman.

He didn't dislike Marissa, or for that matter most of his dad's girlfriends. For the most part they were always nice women, with a few exceptions, and they were kind toward Isaac. He tried his best to befriend all of them the best he could. By this point in his age, none of them took a mothering role with him, but more of the "cool aunt who lets you drink" role.

He vaguely remembers as a child his dad's few "real" girlfriends, the ones who thought they would marry him and were over the moon about having a step-son. Isaac remembers being ecstatic over having a mom, but after years of waiting and watching, he knew not to hope for anything.

He watched as Marissa began the process of making her brownies, lightly humming a song to herself.

Isaac reached over and grabbed a handful of chocolate chips from her bowl.

Marissa faked a small gasp and stern look, "Hey, watch those hands, mister!" She swat at his hand, trying to get him to drop the chocolate chips.

Isaac laughed, backing his way back into the hallway. "This will be my treat to hold me until they're actually done. Thanks, Marissa!" He called back to her as he walked back into the living room.

He heard her chuckle before calling back, "Yeah, yeah, whatever! Don't fill up too much before dinner."

These moments he could live in forever. Pretending that everything was normal. That nothing bad would happen. He hated how he seemed to constantly be waiting for the other shoe to drop when it came to his dad. He may have hated this place, hated moving, hated every way his dad ended his relationships, but he loved the small, tiniest bits of normalcy he got. He loved pretending that whatever woman his dad was with would stay. That he would have someone more reliable than his own dad. That there would be a woman, like Marissa, who would cook and bake for him and joke with him and be someone in his life who stayed. That his dad wouldn't royally fuck up another woman's life.

But he knew it was hopeless. No matter how much he dreamed or hoped or prayed, he knew it would never happen. He was content with pretending for now. He's been pretending his whole life, he could do it for a few years more.

Later that evening, his father returned home, and Isaac was able to pretend some more. The three of them sat together, eating the meal Marissa cooked of course, and he could feel himself pretending they were a real family.

"How was everyone's day?" Marissa asked, holding her hand in front of her mouth as she chewed.

Isaac shrugged, "Just the same old," he looked down at the plate of food. "Started another book."

"Oh, that sounds great. You'll have to tell me about it once you finish it. What about you, honey?" Marissa asked, looking over at Isaac's dad.

He grunted, shoving a piece of food in his mouth. "Work was awful. These idiots don't know what they're doing. The boss keeps hiring these young assholes who don't know jack shit. Expect me to teach 'em." The last part was almost indecipherable as he spoke with the food in his mouth.

Isaac wanted to groan aloud. His dad never seemed to be able to talk about the good. Part of him wanted to apologize to Marissa, but she didn't seem phased. She simply nodded and apologized to his dad, stating that she wished his day had gone differently.

Isaac was able to pretend for a moment that this was his family and that this was permanent. He knew in the back of his head that in a few months his dad would grow bored and would find a woman that excited him. He would start sneaking around. Isaac knew all the signs by this point, and then Marissa would find out, and everything would come crumbling down. He knew it would. His dad always messed up. He tried his best to savor these moments before the inevitable happened.

Isaac thanked Marissa for the meal and she smiled at him and gently reminded him about dessert. He smiled softly and nodded back, making a mental note in his head to get some of the brownies later. He took the stairs two at a time as he went up to his room. He sighed as he sat at his desk facing the window and saw how the rain was still steadily pouring down.

He used to love when it would rain at their old place. It was always refreshing and he enjoyed staying in and watching the rain fall. But now, after months of dealing with almost non-stop rain, he could feel it filling up inside him. It made pretending that everything would work out that much harder.

After much time watching the rain fall and attempting to distract himself with the book he was currently reading, he decided to head downstairs to get the brownies Marissa had made. He thought maybe those would boost his mood even the smallest amount. As he began to make his descent down the steps, he heard the yelling voices. He stopped dead in his tracks, his blood running cold. This was way too soon. His dad surely couldn't have messed up already. Isaac wanted to join in on the yelling, wanted so badly to have his dad know what he thought.

"You think I wouldn't find out?" Isaac heard his dad yell which quickly caught him off guard. What would his dad be finding out about?

"You're never home! It's only ever me and Isaac! Of course I needed something more. I was so lonely. You moved here to be with *me*, not to work," Marissa said, her voice cracking at the end.

"So you make yourself feel better by cheating on me?" His dad's voice echoed through the entire house, and Isaac winced.

"At least it finally got your attention. David, do you know how much it hurt going to bed alone every night because you couldn't pull yourself from your work for two goddamn seconds?"

Isaac heard shuffling and then the clattering of a plate on the table. "Someone has to pay the bills around here. Yes, I moved up here for you, but I still have to work. Be an adult and get used to it or that new guy you're fucking is going to disappoint you too," his dad said coldly.

Marissa sobbed. "He actually cares about my time." He heard her begin walking the other direction, toward the front door. "It's not only my time you've been wasting, David. Isaac deserves a better father than whatever you have going on." Then he heard the door open and slam shut.

A beat after he heard his father let out a yell occupied by the sound of glass shattering. Isaac could hear his heart beating, unsure of what to do next. After counting to twenty and the house remained silent, he slowly made his way into the kitchen where his dad was. Isaac saw him bent over the counter, his head in his hands. By his feet were the shards of glass of a now shattered plate.

"Dad..." Isaac nervously spoke up, taking slow careful steps towards him.

His dad looked up. "Isaac..." He looked down at the glass by him and stepped over it, taking his son into a tight embrace. "I'm so sorry, Isaac. I shouldn't have moved us here. I really thought she was the one."

Isaac listened as his dad let apologies spill out of his mouth. He apologized for moving them here, for moving in with Marissa, for trusting her, and for having Isaac around her. Isaac softly rubbed his dad's back, repeatedly saying it was okay. It wasn't, but there was no point in telling his dad that.

Isaac couldn't help but feel hopeful. His dad was somehow finally getting a taste of his own medicine. Maybe this was the wake up call that he needed. Finally, his dad would see the pain that he had been causing to others for so long and would be a changed man. Isaac knew deep down that this was meant to happen. His dad needed this push, and Isaac was glad that it was Marissa to do it. Isaac almost smiled at the thought of his dad finally snapping out of it and settling down for real, with or without a woman. All he wanted was for him to be a *dad*.

His dad pulled out of the embrace and rubbed Isaac's shoulder. "We're gonna get through this, bud. We always do."

Isaac nodded. "You're right. Let me help clean up and then maybe we can—" The sound of his dad's phone ringing cuts him off. They both glance at it on the counter and his dad quickly snatches it up.

"Get this all cleaned up, would you? I gotta take this." His dad answers the phone and briskly walks into his office, shutting the door behind him.

Isaac swears he saw the glimpse of a picture of a woman taking up the screen.

Brink of Infinity
Mitchell Junious

"I guess this is the end," Bradley thought to himself as he lay on the half-singed ground around him. Naturally, he had heard all the theories of what would happen when he finally met his end, from everyone trying to scare him in basic training. Now it seems like he will know the truth once and for all. No life flashing before his eyes. Maybe because he did not have much of a life or at least did not think much of it since the war started. He did not see the pearly gates or see his soul leaving his shell of a body behind. He did however see a bright light. Not blinding like he imagined it would be, but bright enough to get his attention and silhouette the figure of Mary, his Mary, just as he remembered her: curled auburn hair, piercing eyes, and the inconspicuous beauty mark just below the dimple of her left cheek. But why was she here, in this chaotic hell? Is it even worth questioning at this point? Best to just enjoy these last few moments of consciousness. He closes his eyes to welcome her warm embrace.

"Bradley," she calls out to him. "Bradley."

Then a panicked soldier's voice, "Bradley!"

He snaps back to the war happening around him. Bullets whiz by his head. Shrapnel bounces off the lieutenant's arm standing over him. "Bradley! Are you hit?"

Bradley checks his chest for potential holes, then his hand immediately clasps his wrist making sure his watch is still there. The watch was given to him as a wedding gift. The simple white-faced timepiece survived two previous wars and was owned by three men in his family. Although no one foresaw it going off to battle again, Bradley wanted more than anything for it to survive for another generation.

He manages a nod to his officer.

"Look alive then," says the lieutenant as he hoists the almost certainly shell-shocked Bradley to his feet. All around them, soldiers' gunshots are blaring, the air is thick with dirt blasted into the air by mortars and exploding land mines. Some soldiers fight hand to hand, some are just trying to survive. "We got these Nazi bastards on the run! Only three more kliqs! We gotta keep pushin' to the—"

Boom! The lieutenant's rally is silenced by a Bouncing Betty. Bradley goes down, covered in dirt and blood. He tries wiping the crimson goo from his eyes so he can at least see. He starts to panic. Sounds are muffled. And then...black.

***

Calmness. Birds. Bradley's still body. He tries to open his eyes, but the sunlight burns. He feels around: a boulder, dirt, grass. The light burns his sensitive eyes, but he lifts his head to try to get his bearings. As he forces his eyes open, indistinct shapes and colors start forming around him. He makes out the trees, as far as he can see. "The woods?" he thinks. A low rumble, from behind him, breaks the tranquil sounds of nature. He turns around to see a small dirt road. He moves towards it trying to make out the source of the sound, but it is too far away for him to recognize.

"Get down." And just like that, he finds himself on the ground once more. He struggles for a moment. The man holding him down does not struggle at all; it is clear to both men that Bradley is no physical match. "Say anything and I'll make sure it's the last thing you ever say."

Bradley understands the man's words but can't quite place his accent.

"Tap twice if you understand me," the man continues.

Bradley feels the barrel of the gun dig deeper into the back of his head. He taps the ground twice in compliance.

"I have to check to see if they're still out there so I'm going to let you up. But if you try anything, and I mean ANYTHING, remember what I said before."

Slowly he gets off of Bradley, who in turn picks his head up to get a look at his assumed captor. As the man looks over the boulder towards the road a stream of possible scenarios rush through Bradley's mind: he's too big to overtake, armed so running is out of the question, and whatever he is looking at could be real trouble.

Bradley gives the man a once over so he can see who he's up against. His uniform has no patches to tell rank and his boots are so worn the leather is barely holding together at the binding. All common details among the typical infantryman. His gun hand, however, is completely covered in semi dried blood. Not a good sign to Bradley.

The man mutters to himself, inaudible to Bradley then quickly ducks back behind the boulder. Whatever the man saw, Bradley can tell it spooked him.

He ducks back down, points the gun at Bradley, and puts a finger to his lips, signaling for utter silence. He mouths the words "they're coming" to Bradley.

Bradley's heart races. He can hear it pounding against his chest walls. He looks down at his watch counting the seconds which seem to move as slow as minutes, then back up at the gun that's still pointing at him. He feels individual beads of sweat start to form and trickle down his brow. Then he hears footsteps, faintly in the distance, but approaching their direction. He can't make out how many, but surely enough to easily overtake the two men if they were to be found behind the boulder.

Low chattering joins the footsteps as the group gets closer; close enough to see their shadows from behind the boulder.

"*Did you hear that,*" one from the group says in German. "*I see it,*" another says. "*Shhh, I'm going to get it.*"

There is silence. Bradley and the man look at one another, not knowing what is going to happen.

BANG! A rifle shot goes off.

The man reaches over and puts his hand over Bradley's mouth and pushes the gun against his throat, reinforcing his crystal-clear message.

They hear cheering from the other side of the boulder. "*What was it?*" one asks.

"*A rabbit! We will eat well tonight. I killed it. You can figure out who will cook it.*"

The man and Bradley stay frozen, listening to the cheering battalion, until they are certain they have walked a safe distance away. The man notices Bradley staring at his bloodied hand. "You lost a lot of blood. Something sharp got you in the back of your head, almost bled out, I didn't know if you would make it," he says. Bradley goes to feel the back of his head to confirm the wound.

Before he can, the man grabs his hand. "Don't! The stitches are still fresh," he shouts.

"Who are you?" Bradley asks.

"Heindel," he responds. "We have to go."

"What are you, a medic?"

"I said we have to go."

"I'm not going anywhere until you tell me who you are."

He holds the gun, threatening Bradley. "I said we have to get going." The man cocks his gun.

"And *I* said I'm not going until you tell me who you are."

Both men are taken aback by Bradley's challenge. Silently, they try to conceive their next move. The man uncocks the gun and turns away. Thinking his skepticism may have been out of place and not wanting to further offend the man who saved his life, Bradley starts to stand up, but before he can:

"A few months ago, I was stationed in western France," he starts. "My friend got shot. We carried him to a nearby cottage. He was barely holding on. I still remember the blood—so much it left a small pool in the dirt every time we stopped to catch our breath. When we finally found someone in the village to help, he was already dead. A woman tried to help, but there was no use. She offered to let us stay there, but he had to keep moving."

Thinking of the man's lost reminds Bradley of his own lost in this war. Of Mary. "I lost someone too," Bradley tells him.

"Before we left. The woman gave me something that could've helped if, God forbid, something like this happened again," he says, reaching in his side pocket. He takes out a rudimentary sewing kit. Bradley is stunned. "I didn't think that it would really come in handy, but..." He taps the back of his head, referring to Bradley's wound.

"So, what you're saying," says Bradley. "Is that I'm just a ragdoll."

The two men's laughter breaks the ever-growing tension.

"I'm saying that I'm Friedrick. Gunter Friedrick." He offers a handshake.

Bradley accepts the truce. "Bradley."

"We should get moving. More of them should be coming," says Gunter, as he helps Bradley to his feet.

The two men walk into the nearby forest, periodically stopping to rest, but never for long, lest they be discovered by the ever-searching enemy troops, until they hear a trickling sound in the distance.

"There's a stream ahead. We should stop for water. I'm almost out," Gunter says.

"Go ahead, I'll wait here."

Gunter helps Bradley prop himself against a fallen log, out of sight from the main path they are following.

As soon as Gunter gets out of earshot, Bradley hurries to his feet. Using a nearby branch, he brushes away the imprint in the leaves, where he was sitting, along with a few of his footprints leading to his makeshift hiding spot.

He takes off in the opposite direction, trying his best to cover his tracks so he won't be followed. With no recognizable landmarks in sight, he keeps trekking through the woods, not quite sure if he's going towards civilization, but sure that he is escaping his would-be savior.

"Bradley," he hears a familiar woman's voice call out from the distance. The distraction causes him to trip over a loose vine, crashing face first onto the hard ground, making him lose consciousness.

***

Water pours onto Bradley's face waking him up. He tries to scream out, but a piece of rope in tied around his mouth prevents any word from escaping. Quickly he realizes that not only is his mouth gagged, but his arms and legs are restrained by rope as well.

"Stay calm," he thinks to himself. "Get up."

Mustering up the maximum momentum, flings his body into an upright seated position.

"What were you thinking?" a distinctly accented voice says over him.

Bradley looks up and sees Gunter standing over him.

"In the middle of enemy territory, who knows how far from safety, and you try to run away from the only person who, not only saved your life, but is trying to get you out of this place. Why would you be so stupid?"

Bradley only stares back at Gunter, as he rants.

"Now I have to go back and try to get more water and drag you on top of that. Or do you think you can walk this time without breaking loose like a wild animal?" He stops to compose himself, not acknowledging Bradley. "Good news, I found a body in the woods. There were some supplies that we can use. "I think I saw a map of some kind in his bag," Gunter says as he turns to look through the bag.

Bradley's eyes dart back and forth, not focusing on anything. A bad habit he recently started catching himself doing when the gears of his brain starts churning. With his tied hands behind him, he reaches into his waistband. "Still there," he thinks. He pulls out a bone-handled razor and flips it open, while Gunter is preoccupied. Vigorously, he slides the blade of the razor back and forth against the rope, trying to cut through. He feels the inside of his hands getting wet and the handle getting slippery. He does not know if it is from sweat or if he nicked his wrist with the blade. Either way he knows he has to keep going.

"There are some crackers and dried meat in here if you're hungry." Gunter turns around just as Bradley feels the sharp blade pass through the last fiber of the rope.

"Did he tell my hands are free? Did I make too much noise?" Bradley thinks to himself as Gunter stares at him and finally shakes his head to indicate "no."

Gunter goes back to looking in the bag. Slowly and as quiet as he has ever been in his life, Bradley stands up and creeps towards Gunter, razor in hand, ready to attack.

"Here we are," Gunter says, taking an old worn map from the bag, just in time for Bradley to collide with him, knocking him to the ground. The two tussle and roll around in the dirt, one trying to overpower the other, but neither quite able to gain an advantage. It happens so fast that neither man can fully comprehend their actions, subconsciously relying on only their instincts and reflexes. Bradley gets a hand free and takes a swipe at Gunter's with the blade. Gunter stops it from slicing clear across his face, catching Bradley at the wrist.

His surprise attack has failed, and Gunter cannot be beaten in this test of strength. Out of the corner of his eye, Bradley spots a way out. He manages to scoot the scuffle to his right, just a few inches. The blade inches closer to his face. With another burst of stamina, he scoots them a few more inches. Gunter pushes the razor closer to Bradley's face. As he fights back, keeping the blade from carving into his face with one hand, he stretches his free arm as far as humanly possible, then farther, making his elbow all but pop out of its socket. His fingers quiver almost able to grab a stone, as the blade scrapes against his chin, leaving a thin red line behind.

The combination of the unbelievable sharpness of the razor, and the adrenaline coursing through his veins, completely numbs the pain and feeling of blood dripping down Bradley's neck. It keeps his focus on his current target as his hand is finally able to clutch the smooth exterior of the stone and swing it with all of his might into Gunter's temple, knocking him off.

Gunter, with his exceptional stature, is rocked; a man of smaller stature would have been rendered completely unconscious. Nonetheless, Bradley seizes the window of opportunity and dives to the ground. Gunter regains his composure and orients himself for a second attack with the razor. Bradley, though, comes up with Gunter's gun, and points it right at him. And they both know that gun beats blade every time.

"Tell me what the hell is going on," Bradley says in a much darker voice.

"You need to calm down," Gunter says, trying to de-escalate the situation.

"Don't tell me what I need to do! Who are you?"

"You're confused," he says, slowly inching towards Bradley. Let's just talk about this."

"Don't move again. Who are you?"

"Oberjäger Gunter Friedrick—Bradley cocks the gun, cutting him off.

"Are you insane?"

"Do you want to test that, or do you want to tell me who you really are?"

"I just told you. What more do you—" BLAM!

The bullet hits Gunter's leg. He screeches in pain as he goes down the ground.

"Let's get something straight," Bradley says, standing over Gunter, gun in hand. "If you told me that enlisted men get to walk around with custom guns with fancy wood-engraved handles, well, I'd have to just call bullshit on that one. But here I am with a German man telling me he's a spy for the allies, carrying a custom Kongsberg." Bradley cocks the gun again, keeping it aimed at Gunter. "I have to say, it is a damn straight shooter Oberjäger. Now who are you?"

***

A scientist rushes around a corner, leading to the main laboratory. He resists a full-on sprint, but his short legs can't carry his rotund body fast enough. Another lab assistant notices his freneticism.

"What's wrong, Max? You look like you're about to have a heart attack."

Max keeps walking, ignoring his peer.

The assistant grabs his shoulder, trying to get him to stop. "Did you hear me? What's going on?"

"The Colonel is on his way," Max says. "We haven't improved the results at all."

He keeps moving forward as if on a mission, leaving the dumbfounded assistant suddenly trying to look busy. As Max continues on his way to the lab, he leaves behind him a trail of scientists, low-ranking enlistees, and other personnel, all in fear of the inevitable terror, after he tells them what is in store.

At the lab, a larger-than-life Tesla-esque obelisk stands in the middle of the room, circled by desks and worktables as if the scientist worshipped the device as a technological god. The oddity of the discharges emitted from the peak of the structure is minimized in strangeness by the base, where a group of men are closely gathered around, all scribbling on clipboards and notepads. The base has a dark vortex, contained behind a glass door for the scientists to look through, that appears to be sucking in energy from anything in close proximity. The purpose is unclear other than to power the electrical expulsions.

"What are you doing?" Max yells from the doorway. Running directly to a cage of lab rats near the base of the central machine, he takes a small treat out of his pocket for the rats before continuing to scold the room of workers. "He's almost here, and you're all just standing around?!"

"Is this a bad time," a voice from behind him says in a calm tone.

Max turns to see the Colonel.

"Of course, if it is not, I would love to see some of the progress so far," he says as he walks past Max to the main attraction in the room.

Frozen in fear, there is nothing Max can do but wait, and hope for the best...whatever that may be.

The Colonel walks around the device, carefully inspecting every inch, his gaze not missing the smallest of details, while still keeping a safe distance from the pull of the machine. His gaze turns from the device to the small cage of lab rats near Max.

"I've always been fascinated with rats, especially your rats."

"I don't follow, sir."

"Day in and day out, you poke and prod them, poison them, kill them. Each day another one of their rat family and friends leaves and never returns. Yet through the grief, the pain, and the near certainty that it's just a matter of time until they are next, they just keep going."

Then, as if prepping for surgery, the Colonel starts to remove his black leather gloves, and carefully removes the lid to the rat's cage. He slides his arm in and waits for one of the rats to climb on.

"No biting...no scratching..."

Max's palms start to sweat. The Colonel steps closer to the viewing window at the base of the machine.

"Come professor."

Max shuffles to stand beside the Colonel.

"How long have you worked on the Infinity project?"

"Two years."

"And what have we learned so far?"

He takes a deep breath, then cautiously starts to explain. "The subje—"

The Colonel holds up a hand, halting the words from escaping Max's mouth. "Officially...our last debrief was three months ago" he says pointing to the logbook on a table near Max. Max picks it up and thumbs through a few pages before reading.

"...three weeks after the anomaly first appeared..." he trails off looking at the machine, still seeming to pull energy to its core.

"Stay focused professor," says the Colonel.

"Subjects were responding based on data inputted from the control surface. Once data was inputted subjects had zero percent response rate to outside stimuli and only acted based on inputted data. Data pushed up to ten times the normal human capabilities in strength, dexterity, and endurance thresholds. After the initial successful trial of subject MZ-427's, extended trials began. During the first extended trial, unexpected brain activity was detected in the amygdala and prefrontal cortex shortly before..."

"Professor, we don't have all day."

"Cause of the additional brain activity has been consistently unexplainable. After brain activity spikes, there is a one hundred percent result of subject expiration."

"And what do we know unofficially?"

"Infinitely anomalous, sir."

"A Promethean gift capable of winning the war, and changing humanity's very existence, and all that can be said is 'infinitely anomalous'. Fix this or move to the next phase of testing by next week. I'll expect a full report on my desk in two weeks."

"Sir, we don't have enough answers to move forward. There is no telling the price that we will have to pay for miscalculations. It seems that we will just have to pay the ferryman."

"Two years. That is how long you've had. The full life of a rat. And still no improvements."

In one cold motion, the Colonel flings the rat that he has been holding into the center of the Infinity Machine. The rat floats in the empty space for a few moments. A look of uncertainty turns to one of hope as Max watches the suspended rat.

"Well done professor."

The Colonel turns to leave. Max breathes a sigh of relief.

Then, a cracking sound comes from the Infinity machine. The Colonel turns back to see what is going on. Max looks on in horror. The rat's body starts to twist and contort. It's blood stains the white fur. Max and the other scientists can only watch with dread. Eventually, even the whimpering ceases and the rat's body vanishes. Silence and uncertainty take the air out of the room.

"It seems your congratulations was premature, professor."

In a final act of acceptance, Max reaches into his pocket for another treat.

"There there old friends. It'll all be over soon," he says, dropping the treat in the cage for the mourning rats.

"That it will professor."

With an effortless, callous motion, the Colonel's boot pushes Max Von Strauss into the base of the device. His body is suspended in space as the room of scientists looks on as the rats did.

"God Speed," the Colonel say before exiting to the unsettling symphony of Max's screams and the cries of his colleagues.

Amongst the disturbed people, a young Gunter Friedrick shoves a few important papers into his briefcase in the back corner of the room with no rhyme or reason. Once they are in good enough not to fall out but not well enough to even come near being organized, he exits the room, leaving only the memory of Max and the sounds of his newly mourning comrades behind him.

***

"It was only my third week at that site. All of my years as a scientist, even the worst things I was a part of couldn't prepare me for that moment. I knew that not everything that I did was ethical, even morally right, but...seeing Max like that. Someone who had welcomed me to his department and who truly believed that his work could lead to the advancement of—and then to see him just...destroyed; like something so insignificant."

He stops talking, trying to keep any more of his emotions from coming out.

"Do you have any idea of what that kind of betrayal can do to a person—"

"What is that?" Bradley asks, looking off into the brush.

Gunter looks past Bradley but sees nothing. "What is it?" he asks, gripping a nearby rock for makeshift protection. "Give the gun back."

Bradley ignores him and starts walking towards the bushes.

"Bradley! Get back here!" he says, hoping no one else is around to hear.

"Do you see it?" he asks, still walking to the bushes.

"No! Stop—you're going to get us killed!"

Bradley moves aside a few branches and steps through the bushes.

"GET BACK HERE NOW!" Gunter exclaims.

Bradley ignores him, still focused ahead of him. He takes a few more steps forward. He sees the unmistakable auburn hair from his past.

"Mary—" before he can finish his sentence, or get any closer to his long-lost love, his face meets the ground again. He looks back to see what caught his foot.

"What the hell...?"

He starts sweeping away the leaves in the ground, uncovering a thick cable. He traces it down all the way to the base of a tree.

"Bradley," he hears Mary say behind him. "What are you doing?"

"Mary! I don't know what this place is, but we have to leave now!"

"Calm down," she says.

"No, we have to move."

Bradley grabs her by the arm and starts to pull her through the woods. She resists.

"Bradley, wait! Your head!"

He touches the back of his head and inspects the blood. She does the same.

"Bradley," she says in a calm, cold voice. "What is your mission?"

"I don't know."

"This isn't good."

She takes out a custom Kongsberg and shoots him just below the eye.

As he lays dying, he watches Mary walk behind the tree and start talking into a phone handset.

"Professor? Infinity has failed. Subject's background was integrated too strongly in the programming phase. It caused hallucinations, lack of focus, and ultimate failure of completion...I'll be ready, sir."

Gunter hangs up and walks back to Bradley.

"What a shame. I thought you would last."

He puts two bullets in his head and drags him to a nearby hole: a mass grave for the other failed subjects.

***

The colonel hangs up the phone in the lab.

"Send in another," he announces.

Two lab technicians roll in a body on a gurney, dressed in an American uniform. They probe him, taking notes and injecting careful amounts of experimental drugs. Then they fire up the Infinity Engine. The colonel gives them a nod. In response they dump the body in, and it is gone.

"Infinity will rise," says the Colonel as he leaves the lab.

The Birthday Party
Gillian Laird

My life is about to change. I can feel it in my bones, in the way the wind whistles through my hair as I drive towards the sunset, windows down. With the music roaring, my nerves drown out as they try to tie me into knots over what the other drivers to my left and right must be thinking about me. I try harder to ignore them. And I open my mouth to swallow the colors above—amethyst and topaz, garnet and sapphire. A mine of possibility.

Tomorrow is Thursday, and I will turn twenty-two. I am throwing a birthday party this weekend. I haven't had one in a while because I have been taking lots of drives. And I tend to drive when I feel alone. Something about the tires rubbing against the road, carrying me nowhere, helps me to feel like I have a reason to be on this precipice. Each sky I have driven beneath has felt like a new friend. And the one I drive beneath this evening, on the dusk of my 22nd birthday, feels like a best friend, one who champions me to finally jump off the cliff of my comfort—the cliff I have felt myself balancing on for so many years.

I ease my car to a stop, the red traffic lights beaming through my windshield, and I turn my radio down. Turn it back up, turn it back down. Turn it off. Roll my windows up. My hand falls from the sun-damaged steering wheel and into my lap. It twitches towards my phone in the cupholder. I don't usually like to bother with texting or scrolling or aimlessly looking for something to pass the few moments that a stoplight might keep me, but before I left my house, telling my parents that I wouldn't be gone long, I texted out birthday invitations to the people in my life. I battled for days with the idea that there aren't enough of them left to warrant throwing a party. Then I realized that I never cared about numbers before. I was just grateful to have authentic people by my side, so I sent the invitations and got in the car.

The light turns green, and I pull my hand back to the wheel. Then I turn right. I have a clearer view of the sky going this way. Less trees. I figure that the low-sitting sun is trying to tell me that I should give it more time, that I should give my friends more time to respond. I take a deep breath, turn my music back on, and agree. There is no need to worry. My friends will answer eventually. But it's the answers that I'm scared of. I don't really want proof that I'm the one who made a mistake. Proof that I made a big mistake.

But that's about to change. I can feel it. I'll be twenty-two tomorrow, and I'm throwing a birthday party.

Above, the city water tower looms. Open pastures of emerald grass spread out on either side of the road. Ahead, a line of traffic forms as cars try to turn into a church parking lot, their break lights now almost brighter than the sun itself. I'll probably drive around the block and head home, but for a moment I do think about flicking my blinker to match everyone else's. Church sounds nice, like maybe it could help. I decide to check my phone. But I forgot to use my brakes, so I nearly slam into the car in front of me.

Jesus. Maybe I should go to church. My friend Sadie would definitely agree with that. So, I hit my blinker and wait my turn to enter the parking lot. That's when I see that she is the first person to respond to my invitation. I told her to bring her boyfriend to the party, thinking that would make her more likely to show up. She really loves her boyfriend. At least that's what she tells me when we manage to run into each other at our college campus.

Teeth buried in my lip, I set my phone in my lap, deciding to check her message once I park.

Finding a small spot, I pull into it. But I'm a little too close to the car on my right, so I pull out and try again. Then I'm too crooked. I leave it alone. I make sure my car doors stay locked. I know this is a church parking lot, therefore it's inherently safe—Sadie would think so—but I'm not fond of taking risks.

I reach for my phone again, the screen lighting up my face, and I click on Sadie's message. "Hey," I read. "So happy to hear that you're celebrating..." A smile tugs at my lips. I start to bite my thumb nail. "But I have this thing for my internship—"

I close my phone before I finish reading. It makes a thud when I drop it back into the cupholder, and a few old coins (pennies mostly) rattle beneath the weight. For a while my vision goes out of focus, and when I come back from that placeless place I go to, my contacts have dried out. So, I run my index finger over each eye to adjust them. On the dashboard, my mileage has reached 96,667. I take the 666 as an angel number—a sign of goodwill from the universe that I should remain hopeful about the rest of my friends' responses. I can feel it in my bones.

I'll be twenty-two tomorrow, and I'm throwing a birthday party.

But I'm definitely not dumb enough to stay in a church parking lot with a number like 666 following me around. I take it as a sign to leave. Besides, there's way too many people funneling into the building anyway, and I don't want to make myself uncomfortable by having to sit next to any of them in the pews.

I get back out on the road. Almost immediately, my phone begins to ring. Picking it up, I decide to drive straight instead of turning to go around the block like I originally planned. The sun still has a little longer to be up, just barely on the horizon.

"Howdy," I say as I drive deeper into the countryside, trying to sound cool. Trying to sound quirky.

"Hey," Taylor singsongs. Her bright smile greets me. I smile back before making sure to keep my eyes on the road. My headlights flutter on. I hear another voice on the phone. I realize it's her college roommate, Anne.

Taylor goes to school five hours away, but she's still the closest thing to a best friend I have. We spend summer and winter breaks together.

"What do you need?" I ask. I hope I know exactly what she needs.

"You aren't going to be happy."

Oh.

"I actually have a concert the same day as your party. I know I said that I might be able to make it home to celebrate, but Anne and I have had these tickets since this time last year," Taylor explains. I can tell she is upset. But not that upset.

"This concert really means a lot to me. This singer's, like, a best friend to me, you know. That's how much I love him."

In a different lifetime, Taylor and I would have been going to this concert together.

"I could reschedule my party—or something," I murmur, heat rushing to my cheeks. For once, I'm grateful for the encroaching moon and night sky because the darkness means Taylor can't see how upset I really am.

"No, don't do that! I won't let you," Taylor snaps, her raspy voice sounding dignified, as if it's her personal responsibility to take care of me and make sure I don't cancel my party. "Still invite some girls over, wear your PJ's, and watch a movie! Take cute pictures! It'll be fun! By the way, your gift is supposed to come in sometime next week!"

I don't like that every one of her sentences seems to end with an exclamation.

"Okay," I say.

A beat of silence passes between us.

"I better go. I'm driving."

"Okay!" Taylor says.

I've never been happier to hang up the phone. Just as I thrust it into the passenger seat, my headlights catch on a STOP sign, one I nearly blow through because somehow, I'm devastatingly exceeding the speed limit. I slam on the brakes, and all my stuff flies forward. Once my seatbelt unlocks, I lean down to pick my phone up off the floorboard.

Taking a few deep breaths, I turn the radio back on and drive. I'll be twenty-two tomorrow, and I'm throwing a birthday party.

The moon is now high and full, and I wish I had just driven around the block and gone home like I planned. I think about texting my friends that I met online a few years ago. We talk all the time, so they're real—not creepers or anything. I doubt they'll come all the way here on such short notice (they're both from other states), but I decide to message them each an invitation anyway.

As I'm doing that, my friend Demie texts me. We met during my sophomore year of college. At the time, her boyfriend had just broken up with her, but now they're back together, so I told her she could bring him to my party. Her message reads, "Is Michael going to be there?"

Shit. I knew I should have asked her before I invited him. We all used to be friends, but Michael liked Demie in a way that Demie didn't like Michael. Now none of us talk much anymore.

In the sky, the moon's silver glow seems to flicker, goading me.

"I did invite him, but he hasn't responded," I quickly type back.

Little more than a second passes before she messages back: "Now that I'm back with my ex, I think I would feel really uncomfortable with that. Sorry."

I knew better. Should have seen this coming. But then, as if fate is listening, Michael and several more of my friends respond.

Alas:

Michael writes, "My co-worker called in sick, gotta fill-in."

Hardin says, "Man, I'm sorry, but I can't make it. I'm taking on an extra shift so I can buy something nice for Elise."

Elise is his girlfriend.

Darius can't come, either. He apparently has work, too.

Summer, the girl I only met because she needed to find someone to take up her babysitting job, can't come to my party either. She has work. At her new job. In an office apparently.

Claire texts, "Wow, look at you! I thought you didn't like your birthday anymore."

My fingers tremble as they type. "I love my birthday. I just haven't had a party in a while because everyone has been so busy since we all went to college."

But it doesn't matter, because Claire can't come—

Before I even realize what has happened, I've crashed into a ditch. My airbags are slapping me in the face and in the side of the head, and my windshield shatters into my lap. I take a long time to sit and breathe, to sit, blink and think. My throat feels very tight. But I don't cry. I never cry.

Instead, I check my phone. It's still perfectly intact, thank the Universe. I can't see the moon anymore, only grass and darkness and the barbed wire fence I've dented with my car. I can see some trees. No other cars drive by. But the moon—I can still feel it watching, so impossibly full.

My phone dings. It's a text from my friend Maya. I told her she could bring her boyfriend to my party. But she can't come. Because she has dinner with her boyfriend's family.

Something wet drops onto my phone, blotting out Maya's contact photo. I think I'm bleeding. Reaching up to touch my forehead, I discover a river of blood, one that paints my fingers with my past, present, and future. Even under the cover of night, I can see the maroon hue, and I can see how it used to be brighter. How it used to be younger. Back when I had friends who cared, friends who didn't have boyfriends. Back when we were all the same.

Back in girlhood.

And I made the mistake of staying there.

I think I'm screaming. I do for a while. But I don't cry.

Because I'll be twenty-two tomorrow.

Mackenzie's First Adventure
Kayla McKinley

An icy chill floated from the frosty windowpanes, causing shivers to run down Mackenzie's back as she carefully crept from her bed to watch as the snowflakes slowly fell from the sky outside. The familiar church bells far in the distance pronounced how late the hour was. As they happily chimed the time, one set of heavy, deliberate footsteps sounded on the stairs in the hall outside Mackenzie's bedroom door.

She hurriedly put on her coat wondering to herself, "*Who would come to visit at this hour?*"

Her apartment was small and there were only a few other tenants that lived in the building. The building was old and drafty but on the plus side it was usually extremely quiet which made it a good place to think and rest-two things that Mackenzie Davison spent a lot of time doing.

Clang! Bang! Clang! An array of short-lived notes made from crashing objects surged through the air. Then, it happened...

"Help!" The shrill cry of an old woman, Mrs. Jones broke the sound of banging and crashing.

Mrs. Jones had been like a grandmother to Mackenzie, always baking cookies and telling stories. In this moment, Mackenzie's heart skipped a beat-but she did not hesitate as she opened her door and stepped into the unprotected hallway. Mrs. Jones' apartment was right next to Mackenzie's and as Mackenzie slowly approached the door that had been left ajar, she stopped. There was a glimmer like a precious jewel in a dark cave deep underground coming from inside Mrs. Jones' apartment. Mackenzie could not make out what it was because of the dreary grayness that made it difficult to see from the hallway. Just before Mackenzie took a step inside, she felt something hard and heavy hit the back of her head and for two seconds she could not see or feel anything but tingling everywhere. And then as the ground beneath her seemed to melt, all went dark.

***

A dim light emerged from the hazy grayness. Mackenzie couldn't move! She then realized that she had been tied to a chair and that she had been kidnapped.

"*But why? By whom?*" Even these simple thoughts made her dizzy as she remembered the events of last night—or was it still the same night? Her sense of time had gone away.

Just as her eyes began to adjust to the dimly lit room, inaudible voices could be heard, and they grew louder and nearer. A rusty, silence-breaking screech broke the sound of voices and a door that Mackenzie had not noticed before began to turn on its hinges.

***

A woman with a long thick coat entered the room and said, "Good evening, Mackenzie. I would like to have a few words with you." Makenzie's surprise was obvious as her lower jaw had dropped, and she was unable to speak.

"First of all, I would like to apologize to you for this inconvenience," the woman said untying Mackenzie from the chair, "You were in grave danger last night. This may come as a surprise, but Mrs. Jones is not who you think she is....She is a thief!"

"A thief!"

"Yes," the lady continued, "she had stolen relics and jewels from Europe and Japan twelve years ago during one of her criminal sprees. And we had just now been able to locate her. She's done this sort of thing before, you know." She glanced back at Mackenzie, then paced a couple of times before sitting back down. "We need your help. She escaped last night. We need your help because you are the only one that can open the safe—the safe that contains old Mr. Ross's inheritance. That man died in 1890 and had no children, so everything he had went to the church and now belongs to the town. The safe is locked, but your late father willed you the key. You were very young when he used to take care of the church, but I think you remember—"

"How do you know so much about me?" Mackenzie interrupted.

"I work for a government agency. I know everything about you and...Mrs. Jones," the woman replied with a grim look, "Besides you don't really have a choice. Mrs. Jones is looking for the key that you have, and she won't stop until she has it. That's why we need to open the safe and relocate the contents."

***

Before dawn, Mackenzie was facing an old church that she did not want to enter, but the authoritative words of the woman from last night stuck in her head and replayed like a broken record: "besides you don't really have a choice..." the woman had said. Those words seemed to control Mackenzie as she stepped near an open window on the right side of the church. Her shoes were completely covered in snow, but she managed to slip into the church without much trouble.

Once inside the room filled with stiff, stale air, Mackenzie felt the weight of her mission. She slowly walked toward the impos-

135

ing staircase, then paused. After a deep breath, she slowly stepped onto the stairs in the way people do when they are trying to avoid the creaking of old flooring. When she finally reached the second floor, she opened the door which still had a sign with her father's name written on it. The sight of the large safe spurred her to action. Mackenzie Davison put the key to the lock and turned it. Click! The door had opened! However, there were no checks, cash, or gold in the safe! Instead, there was a tiny object that glimmered and sparkled brighter than any star Mackenzie had ever seen! And it sparkled exactly like the object in Mrs. Jones' apartment Mackenzie had seen just hours ago.

Mackenzie had accomplished her mission. So, she pocketed the precious gem and began her descent down the stairs. The woman from the government agency met her at the church's front double-doors and gladly accepted the gem from Mackenzie. Mackenzie reluctantly handed the gem to the woman, who eyed it once before putting it in her own pocket.

"Mackenzie, we all owe you a big thanks! You stopped a criminal from stealing this. It will be put in a bank vault and then returned to your hometown where it belongs once Mrs. Jones is no longer a threat. But, if Mrs. Jones had gotten it, she would have sold it illegally to fund more of her villainous schemes. Today, you have become a hero!" she paused then turned back toward Mackenzie, "Actually, Mrs. Jones is still on the run. How would you like an official job as an agent? What do you say? Would you like to join our team?"

Mackenzie grinned, "That sounds exciting! Count me in!"

Countdown
Christine Osborne
Sanderson Award for Fiction

A classroom stretches ahead of me, a long lecture hall that never seems to reach the front. Behind me, the tick tick tick of the Doomsday Clock counts down to my demise. A tick tick tick that I can't shake, no matter where in the classroom I move. Every time I switch seats, dodging the judgmental stares of classmates, the front of the classroom never moves closer. First this row, next to Maria, then the next, Omar. I can feel their scathing stares while I putter about, racing against the clock to reach the front, to reach the end. The lecture hall stretches endlessly ahead of me, and the clock counts down my every move. Nothing is changing yet everything feels different, foreign. There's no end to the journey, I'm constantly moving toward a destination that I know will be the end of me, the end of the clock.

I stop in the midst of changing seats, twisting my body to look behind me. I don't know what I expect to see, maybe the clock dogging my every move, but it feels like I've gone nowhere with the short expanse behind me. The faces of my classmates, crammed into ten rows of uncomfortable seats, stare at me with disdain. Omar, Maria, Phillip, that one kid that has allergies year-round. Their scorn bares me, striking deep as their faces morph into those of the people I love. Mom, Dad, Grace.

I can't tell whether they were always there, watching me race to a destination I'll never reach or if my classmates transformed into them. Whatever it is, I feel crippled by their stares. Content to take a seat and wait pacifically for the front to reach me. For the clock to stop ticking and the world to implode. I sit there, in the lightly-padded lecture hall seats with the sticky tables as the weight of the world rests on my shoulders, leaving me helpless in my own life.

***

A sharp trill breaks me from my nap, an incessant noise that won't go away. Groggily opening my eyes as I blink away the film on my contacts, I fumble around to find the source of the noise. My fumbling finally finds something that vaguely resembles my phone in shape, so I grab it and bring it close to my face, squinting in the bright light of the screen and the now-louder ringtone. It's my mom.

I groan and swipe to pick up. I always pick up. "Hello?" My voice is croaky with sleep, and I don't sound too happy to be awake.

Probably because I'm not. Being awake means dealing with responsibilities and people and expectations—all things I prefer not to think about.

"Elizabeth," My mom starts the conversation. I can hear the disappointment in her tone. "You just woke up, didn't you?" I don't respond. "You realize that it's 4 o'clock in the afternoon and you have dinner with your dad in an hour, right? Don't you forget this time or that man won't let me hear the end of it. Not that he ever does." I groan and sit up, my head spinning as I suddenly become half vertical.

"I didn't forget. I was just hoping to sleep through it." I mumble, stumbling to my feet. My limbs and head feel heavy from my long nap, and I don't feel ready to be awake at all.

She huffs in exasperation because she knows my antics. Her tone shifts to concern, "Are you alright, hon? Grace said you haven't been talking to her much this year and when you do, you avoid all her questions..." Now the mom voice, "And don't you dare dodge mine."

"I'm fine, I'm fin—" I try to fob off her question, but it doesn't work.

"Elizabeth Grace Finch," all she says is my full name and I know I'm in for it. I wait for Mom to say more, but she doesn't say anything. Which means it's up to me to tell her what's going on, no hints or help. Thanks Grace.

I sigh and sit back down on my bed, "I'm just tired, Mom. Really tired." I hope that's enough, but when she still says nothing, I have to continue. "I just can't wrap my head around this stuff. Every time I think I have it, it's not right and then I have to spend even longer figuring out where I messed up. It's easier to just sleep and avoid it and find the answers online later."

"Why don't you try something different?" She finally says, offering what might have been a helpful suggestion if I hadn't already tried that.

"I tried. I've been in every science you can think of: biology, chemistry, physics. They're all prerecs. It just...doesn't click. The only way I've made it this far is because of Dr. Google and his friend Señor Chegg."

"Sure, but why not something different?" My mom offers again, as if she didn't just say that.

I roll my eyes even though she can't see me, "I just said that I already tried, Mom."

I'm sure she's rolling her eyes too when she says, "Not like that. Something really different. Not STEM or anything like that, but maybe History—I know how you like history—or English or heck even some business classes. Just—something different from what you're doing. Maybe you'd enjoy it more." She sounds hopeful at the end there, but I'm gonna have to crush her dreams there—or maybe just mine...

"Not to burst your bubble or anything, but you do know that Dad won't let me take that, right? Like you did hear the conditions of him paying for college? Good, cuz, I sure haven't forgotten, especially since one of his conditions happens this Friday night and he won't let me forget it." I'm a little spiteful, but these dinners are truly miserable with him dogging my every move.

"I'm just saying, Elizabeth, that I want you to be happy. I want you to do what makes you happy, and if science makes you miserable, then maybe you should switch, no matter how far you are through." She's resolute, kind.

"And Dad? And the money?"

"I'll take care of him. And as for the money, you're smart." I flinch, I certainly don't feel smart... "You'll find some way to pay for it. I can even help you take out some loans if needed, maybe start building your credit."

"I don't know Mom..." I trail off. All of this just seems too idealistic, too impossible. How could anyone be happy in what they do?

"Just think on it. You do whatever feels best, but just know that I'm in your court, no matter what. I just want you to stay happy and healthy. I love you."

"Love you too. Talk to you later." I hang up the phone and flop back into my bed. That's a lot to think about. Maybe I should just take a nap instead.

I've always thought that money and paying for college was the most important thing, which is why I accepted my dad's offer to cover tuition as long as I went into a STEM field he approved of and met him for dinner one Friday a month to keep him updated. Pretty small terms if you look at the big picture. But in the smaller picture, I'm miserable. I have no friends, no time, and no desire to do anything besides sleep. It's honestly kind of soothing in the times that it doesn't feel miserable. Dad pays for my tuition and gives me an allowance and I can do whatever I want as long as I get my homework done and pass my exams (which happens thanks to Señor Chegg and solution manuals). What more could I want? What more could I expect?

I sigh and toss a pillow at the ceiling idly. It falls back on my face—an apt reflection of my mental state right now. I don't know what to do. Mom's right. I'm miserable. Really and truly miserable and tired and anxious and just really really tired. Sleep beckons, but I know that if I don't figure this out before my dinner with Dad, I'll be stuck in the same loop. The same misery.

I'm two and a half years into my degree—any switch now and I'll be throwing away at least a year's worth of tuition and wasting my credits. But does it matter? Does it matter how much money and time is wasted if it means that I'll be miserable my whole life—trapped in a job I never wanted? I don't think so. No, I know so. I don't know that I've ever seen anyone really and truly happy with their job, but that doesn't mean I can't be. But if I don't make this switch now, it'll be too late, too entrenched. It has to be tonight. I just hope I can stand my ground...

***

"No. Absolutely not," My father declares, staring down at me with his imposing stature. "I did not put thousands of dollars into your education for you to get cold feet halfway through and change fields."

I flinch. He has a point there, and it's nothing I haven't been telling myself for the past few hours as I deliberated over this decision. "But Dad—" I try to get a word in, but he's on a roll now, spewing his self-centered, financial concerns all over my fragile feelings.

"Did your sister do this? No. She went and finished her degree—at Yale for chrissakes, and you can't even finish your tiny little BioChem degree at your I-don't-even-remember-the-name-of-it-half-the-time school!" I'm shrinking with every word he says, trying to make myself a smaller target for his verbal wrath. "Do you know how hard I work for every penny put toward your education? No, of course you don't, because if you did you wouldn't be making this absurd decision and, oh wait, you're not making this decision because it's absurd and if you go through with it, I won't pay a cent more for your education. I can't believe I work my ass off every day, put every fiber of my being into working, so that you can get the life you deserve, and you stab me in the back like this." At his words, I remember exactly why I'm here. Why I'm throwing myself to the wolves for a chance to pursue something I actually enjoy.

"I can't believe your mom raised you like this, because clearly it wasn't me. I would never raise my daughter to make such flippant decisions. I raised you to follow through on your commitments. That woman and I need to have some words." I straighten my shoulders, remembering who I am. I'm not a coward who lets her dad run over her.

"Have you told her? Why do I even ask, of course she knows, she probably told you to do this just to spite me. I should never have let you run off with your mom. That woman is putting ridiculous ideas into your brain. Thank God I kept your sister, she's turned out much better." I face his lecture head on, looking my dad straight in the eyes. I don't back down from confrontation.

I clear my throat, readying to speak. I speak my mind, my dreams. "Fine." I say clearly, bringing myself, my decision, back into the focus of Dad's rant.

He stops. "Fine what? Fine, you'll keep going with your degree?" He sounds almost hopeful.

"No," I'm resolute. I won't back down. "I'm going to switch my major and I'll pay for every cent of it if you won't support me in my dreams. Somehow, I thought you were a better parent than that, but you really only care about what you want, your money, your job, your life. So, screw it." He blubbers, trying to say something, but I'm my father's daughter so I push forward, speaking over him, "I'm tired of you trying to control my life when you're not even in it. You put all of the attention onto Grace and that's fine with me, but I don't want you coming back after the years I spent with Mom and trying to control me just because you're giving me a little money. So, I'm done." I'm breathing heavily, spent emotionally and physically from my outburst. But it feels like a weight has been lifted off my shoulders—a weight to be perfect, to live up to expectations, to do what's expected. I'm done.

***

A lecture hall stretches out before me, rows and rows of folded chairs vacant of students. Miles away at the front of the classroom is the whiteboard with chemistry scribbles indecipherable from this distance. This scene feels familiar, but I can't place it. Instinct —no, habit?—has me taking a step forward, then another. Slowly, I'm walking down the aisle, the too-large steps causing me to gain momentum and speed up. I turn to sit down in an edge seat, but the once-vacant folding chair is now occupied. A glance around shows that all the other seats are filled too. The path that was once open to me is now closed, no seats available.

Students stare at me—the professor too, who wasn't there just a moment ago. I stand alone in the aisle, disoriented, confused, distressed. But instead of the judgement and embarrassment I expect to feel from their stares, I feel nothing.

Something compels me to look behind me, to the back of the vast hall. A large clock hangs on the wall, counting down the minutes until the end of lecture. Counting down the minutes until the end of me. Only, it's not a clock anymore.

The ticking I expect to hear is gone—why did I expect that? There is no clock on the back wall—was it ever there? It must not have been, because there is a door right where I think I just saw a clock. Thin lines of white light radiate around the thick wooden door, beckoning me closer with their shine. I look around. No one is looking at me anymore, the professor lecturing about molecular bonds in a heavy accent as if I had never been there, as if I weren't there right now.

That gives me the push I need to turn around and stride back up the steps, to the shining light at the back of the classroom. The wide steps that sped up my downward trek now slow my upward motion, making every step drag on with the extra energy needed to climb. As I reach the top step, reaching for the handle of the shining door, something stops me in my tracks.

My father's face is projected onto the door, his head profiled in shadows, the memory of his voice and stern expression holding me back. "Don't do this, Elizabeth. You'll regret it."

I won't.

I pull the door open and step through.

The Journey
Savanna Peveto-Kreatschman

Enoch couldn't remember a time when he'd seen such a beautiful sky. He was snapped out of his pleasant observing by the sound of wheels approaching. He looked up, expecting the bus, only to be greeted by a black Cadillac DeVille. The car slowly approached, pulling up right in front of Enoch. He didn't know why, but he knew the car was there for him. He hesitantly got up, opened the door, and slid onto the leather seat. He looked to the driver, seeing the most beautiful man he had ever seen. This man seemed to have a warm, gentle glow around him. He was ethereal, a being of complete perfection. Enoch knew he should be wary of getting into a car with a stranger, but confusingly, he felt at ease, almost like the stranger was an old friend.

Enoch buckled up as the stranger switched gears and started driving.

"Do I know you?" Enoch questioned.

"Well...yes, but it's been a while. The name's Azrael," the stranger replied.

Enoch didn't recall ever meeting Azrael, but he sensed honesty in his words.

"Why are you here?" Enoch asked, immediately regretting his wording as he might take it as rude.

Azrael just chuckled, saying, "I'm here to help of course," as if it's common knowledge.

"I don't understand," Enoch said, his brow scrunching in confusion.

"I'm here to help you with your worries, to talk," he replied.

"Oh," Enoch said, as if it all suddenly made sense.

"Why don't we talk about how you've been feeling recently," Azrael said, briefly looking over at Enoch.

Enoch didn't usually like talking about how he was feeling, as it seemed like that was all people cared about these days when it came to him but coming from Azrael it felt different.

"It's been really hard recently," Enoch sighed, "Ever since my cancer took a turn for the worse, it's like everyone's been on overdrive, trying to make sure I'm always comfortable and have everything I need. I know they're just trying to help, but it's suffo-cating." Enoch turned to Azrael, who nodded at him to continue. Enoch felt heard for the first time in a long time.

"Everyone is so worried about me. My sister is constantly trying to cheer me up with games and jokes. My mom can't stop crying, as if I were already gone. My dad can't even look at me anymore. To them I'm like a walking corpse. They're forgetting me before I'm even gone. If they're hurting this much while I'm still here, I can't imagine how much pain they'll be in when I'm gone. I just wish I could take away their pain. Sometimes I wish I could just hurry up and die so they won't have to keep holding on to the fake hope that I'll get better."

"They love you," Azrael replied, "They just want to help in any way they can."

"But they know I won't. We all know that I'm going to die soon. Each day I can feel my life slowly draining my body, each day I feel less and less like myself. I don't know why they keep pushing me to act like everything's the same as it's always been, like everything's gonna be okay. What are they gonna do when I'm gone, and they can't pretend anymore?" Enoch said hoarsely, tears threatening to spill. Azrael looked at him. Unlike everyone else, he didn't look at Enoch with pity, but with a heartbroken, yet knowing look. Almost as if he actually understood how Enoch was feeling, not just saying he did.

"It's going to be hard for them when you're gone. They're always going to miss you, but eventually they will learn to remember you through the happiest memories and not through the pain they felt losing you. We don't forget those we've lost, just learn to live with the grief as if it were an old friend," Azrael said solemnly. Enoch wanted to argue, to say, what if his family moved on and forgot him? Or worse, what if they were never able to move on? But somehow, he knew Azrael was right, that eventually, after he was gone, everything would be okay.

Enoch closed his eyes, his voice barely a whisper, "I can't even remember what it was like before I was sick, it seems like the whole world was flipped upside down the day I was diagnosed." Enoch closed his eyes, remembering the day everything changed.

***

Enoch had been sick for a couple of weeks. He was constantly throwing up, moody, and tired. His parents had taken him to see so many doctors that he had lost count, up until one doctor could finally give him the right diagnosis.

"I'm so sorry," the doctor said to Enoch's parents, "I'm afraid he has cancer."

"Oh my god," his mother said, breaking into sobs.

"What can we do?" his father pleaded.

"There's not much we can do. It's gotten past the point of reversing the symptoms. We can do treatment, but it will only postpone the inevitable, he's terminal," the nurse said with a look of pity in her eyes.

After that, things were mostly a blur. He remembered his father yelling, his mother taking his sister and him out of the room, and doctors and other nurses trying to calm his father down. After that day nothing was the same. It felt like his days were nothing but school and doctors' appointments, until eventually he got so sick that he no longer went to school. That was when he moved into the hospital, his days reduced to pills, checkups, and bad pudding. Through it all, his family was always there, even when he knew there were other things they needed to be doing. It made him feel like a burden, but he didn't want them to leave. He didn't want to be alone, not in the cold, quiet hospital.

**

"I know it wasn't easy but remember you're still alive. There is still time," Azrael said, bringing Enoch out of his memories.

"Well, we've arrived," he stated as he brought the car to a stop and turned to look Enoch in the eye, "But I need you to remember, just because you know you're going to die soon, doesn't mean you should give up living while you can."

Enoch sat for a moment, letting silent tears trail down his face before unbuckling and stepping out of the car. He looked ahead, seeing a thin blue door with a small window at eye level. Through the gaps in the door, he could see a blinding white light. Despite his fear, he knew that door would take him to where he was meant to be. With one last glance back at Azrael, he made his way to the door. Gripping the cold handle, he walked through the doorway.

Enoch blinked a few times, letting his eyes adjust to the bright hospital lights and sterol room he spent the majority of his days in. He looked around, seeing his mother and sister fast asleep in the chairs beside the hospital bed, and his father standing at the foot of the bed, not looking up at his approach.

"I'm scared," Enoch said to his father.

For the first time in a long time, his father looked at *him*, "Me too."

He opened his arms for Enoch, embracing him tightly. Enoch breathed in his familiar cologne, feeling at home. Safe. This feeling made him realize that, despite how he previously felt, *it was not yet his time.*

The Start
Savanna Peveto-Kreatschman

She felt beautiful, almost powerful as she applied the last bit of her makeup and touched up her hair. She was so excited to go out with her friends to the club. She had been so stressed recently with work and school that it would be a relief to let loose and enjoy herself. She pushed her hair over her shoulder and stood up to grab her coat. She just needed to tell her boyfriend goodbye, then she could be on her way. However, as she walked up to him, his face morphed into one of derision.

"What's wrong?" she asked.

"Nothing, everything's perfect," he stated, his tone dripping with sarcasm.

"Come on, just tell me. What's the problem?"

"Your outfit's the problem," he sneered.

"What's wrong with my outfit," she asks incredulously. She didn't understand the problem. He's silent for a minute. She almost thinks he didn't hear her, until he speaks, "I can't believe you would do this. You know how that makes me feel."

"I don't know what you're talking about!" she exclaimed.

He stood up quickly, the chair scraping against the floor, "I can't believe you want to go out like that!"

"What do you mean? There's nothing wrong with it!"

"You know exactly what's wrong with it! You're just looking for attention. You're upset that I haven't been giving you attention, and you're trying to make me jealous!" he shouted.

"No, that's not what I'm doing. It had nothing to do with you!" She felt like her anger was going to boil over. Everything felt too hot, too confusing. She didn't understand why this was happening, how everything had gotten so out of control so quickly. He ignored her, turning to walk away. She went to grab his arm.

"I'm not done talking to you!" she said, pulling him back. What came next happened faster than she could comprehend. As she pulled him back, he grabbed her wrist, shoving her back roughly, the sound of her head connecting to the wall ringing out into the now silent space. Everything was still for a moment, until the sobs poured out of her. His expression immediately changed into one of shock and fear at what he'd done. He rushed toward her, cradling her face, apologizing over and over.

"Baby, please, I'm so sorry. I didn't even realize what I was doing. I didn't mean to. You know I would never hurt you. I love you so much."

At first she fought against him, pushing against his chest. But, as she started to overcome the shock of what had happened, she was able to think again, to listen. He was so worried about her, panicked really. She could hear it in his voice. The way he whispered her name over and over, like a chant that could turn back time. She could hear the tears in his voice. He would never hurt her, had never hurt her. It was just an accident. Things were just heated, they were yelling and he lost control. He didn't mean to.

She leaned into him, sagging from exhaustion. She felt spent. It was all too much and she just wanted to lay down.

"It's okay," she whispered, "I know you didn't mean it. We're okay."

He wrapped his arms around her, tears falling down his face. He held her too tightly, but she didn't say anything. They went and laid down, and she let him fall asleep wrapped around her. Once his breaths had evened out and his arms had slackened, she wriggled out of his hold, laying down on her back to stare at the ceiling. At first no thoughts came. She laid there listening to him breathe, each break in the steady rhythm had her holding her breath.

Then the flashes came. She replayed what happened in her head over and over again. But the more she went through it, the more muddled it became. And so it continued until she no longer remembered why she had been so panicked and afraid. She knew she should be angry, he hurt her. But she knew him. He would never do anything to hurt her. They had been together for more than three years. If he was abusive, she would have known by now. No, this was just an accident.

This happened because things had gotten out of control. She shouldn't have grabbed him like that. Him pushing her was just a reflex. If she hadn't pulled him then he wouldn't have reacted like that. He wasn't an abuser. She had seen those fliers about abuse, heard about the atrocious acts committed towards those women. He would never do those things to her. He was a good guy.

He was caring and thoughtful. He took off work to take care of her when she was sick. He cooked for her and brought her flowers when work became especially stressful. He was the perfect boy-friend. Her friends and family always told her how lucky she was. She already knew, though. He always went above and beyond to be there for her. He loved her, and she knew that. What happened was just a bump in their relationship. They would get past this and things would go back to how they were before.

As her feelings about the situation settled, she realized she was still in her clothes from the night before. She got up to change, but decided to take a shower first. She felt dirty, tainted. She scrubbed her skin until she lost track of time, until the water turned cold and her skin was raw and tender to the touch, but she still didn't feel clean. She got out of the shower and got dressed. She put on an oversized hoodie and pajama pants. She went back to the room and picked up the outfit from earlier. She stared at the knee length flowy dress for a moment, trying to make sense of the damage it had caused. She went to hang it up, hesitating before tossing it into the trash can instead. She never really liked the color anyway.

The Things We'll Never Do
Savanna Peveto-Kreatschman

I saw her. I saw her in strangers' smiles, in children laughing and playing on the playground. I saw her in the rainy days she loved so much. I saw her everywhere, which only made the pain of losing her worse. My sweet, loving wife.

On the third week after the accident, I visited her favorite coffee shop and ordered the drink she had been begging me to try. She had been asking me to come with her to get coffee for weeks, saying that, despite my strong dislike for coffee, she knew a drink I would love. Even though it was too late, I felt like I owed it to her for all the things we'd never be able to do together. The barista handed me the coffee, a look of pity in her eyes. Of course she knew, everyone knew. It seemed like that same look of pity could be found in the eyes of everyone who knew me. Everyone who knew that I had lost my whole world. I hated that look, like everyone was waiting, expecting me to shatter into a million pieces at any given moment. I waited with them. She was my everything, and without her I am nothing.

I took a sip of the coffee, hating how much I liked the taste. Realizing she was right only made the pain worse. I threw the still full drink in the trash before hurrying back to our house. *My* house.

On the fifth week I got a call from her friend. I was expecting this, but it didn't stop the white ball of hatred from catching in my throat as I answered the call.

"Hello?"

"Hey, how are you doing? I know this has been hard for you, so I just wanted to check and see how you were doing," they asked, only making my hatred grow. Rationally, I knew it wasn't their fault. They couldn't have known what would have happened after calling that night begging for help. They couldn't have known how bad the storm would have gotten, how slippery the roads would have become. But that didn't stop my hatred. I felt like I needed someone to blame, but the only one I should have been blaming was myself. I shouldn't have let her go.

"I'm doing okay," I replied.

"I'm sorry I couldn't stay for long at the funeral, I had to pick my daughter up from daycare. Oh...God I'm so sorry. I shouldn't have said that. I didn't mean to, it's just I wasn't thinking. I know losing both your wife and the baby like that must hurt, and I just—"

"It's okay. It's not your fault," I lied. I felt like I had been slapped in the face, the tears stinging my eyes. I felt so angry. I knew it was just grief, but that didn't make their words hurt any less.

"I know, I just feel bad. Just remember this is all part of God's plan for you, and that all you need to do is have faith that this is how it's meant to be."

"What?" I sat there dumbfounded. I had to have misheard them.

"I know you must miss her a lot. I just wanted to call to let you know that God is with you. This is all part of his plan for—"

"Listen, I'm really busy. Can I call you back some other time?" I interrupted.

"Oh...yeah, of course. Just let me know—"

"Thanks," I hurried, hanging up and throwing my phone on the couch.

On the eighth week her mother came to visit me. I could see the worry on her face. The same sadness I knew my eyes reflected. In this neverending pain, I knew we were the same. We were what she left behind.

"She loved you so much."

"That didn't save her."

We sat in our sorrow, wondering what we could have done to save her, knowing nothing could undo what had already happened. After some time, her mother got up to leave. I stopped her, going over to the almost empty table, grabbing the small square photo from the last ultrasound appointment my wife and I went to before the accident, and handing it to her. She stared at it for a few seconds before breaking into sobs.

"She would have wanted you to have it."

Her mom left after that, tears trailing silently down her face. I felt so immeasurably tired, like all my sadness weighed down on me, fracturing my heart from the size. With her mom gone, the feeling of loneliness returned. It was a small house, always meant to be temporary. It was cluttered with books and random knick knacks. The house was never dirty, just disorganized. She always complained how there was never an empty spot on the table to set anything down, even though it was mostly her things scattered on the table. Now, without her the cluttered house felt so large and empty. I would never again wake up to her dancing and making breakfast. I would never again argue with her that she already had enough books, only to give in and drive her to the bookstore later on. I would never again see her smile that seemed to light up her face every time she saw me. There were so many things that died with her in that car. I died with her in that car.

Another wave of tiredness crashed over me. I headed to the storage closet to grab my bedding and place it back on the couch. I didn't want her mom to see what I had become.

I headed to the bathroom to get ready before bed, pausing at the room before it. I hated this room. It stood as a reminder of everything I had lost that night. I slowly turned the knob letting the door creak open. The pink flowery wallpaper looked faded and lifeless. The small dresser filled with clothes that would never be worn. The little crib sat empty and untouched since the last day we worked on it together. We were so excited to pick out names and plan ultrasound appointments. I closed the door, not able to bear looking at it anymore. It was as if every time I opened that door, *I saw her.*

The Price of Freedom
Savanna Peveto-Kreatschman

It had been a long day, one of the worst May thought as she dragged herself through the doorway of her cramped apartment. Then again, it seemed like everyday had become a long day. May felt battered and worn. Her scrubs were rumpled, her chestnut brown hair escaping the once neat bun in thick strands. Everyday was the same. Wake up. Go to work. Come home. Sleep. Then repeat it all over again the next day.

It hadn't always been like this. As a young girl, May had so much promise. She had straight A's, was team captain of the debate team, and was the favorite of many teachers and peers. She had the perfect life. The perfect family. Her parents always pushed her to do her best. Sure, they were a little strict. They didn't allow her to have social media, date, or even really hang out with friends that often. But they did it for May. They wanted her to succeed, to be the best she could be. May never seemed bothered by her parents' strict expectations and rules. In fact, she always seemed so happy. No one would have ever guessed the secrets she kept hidden behind her perfect smile and neatly put together look.

After showering and dressing in her pajamas May went and sat on the floor beside her bed. She sat there for a minute before reaching under her bed and pulling out a box. It wasn't a very large box, maybe the size of a microwave. It was made out of dark wood with a rusty silver latch that always got stuck, and a handle to carry it around, not that she ever did. It looked like a place to store old antiques, or papers that were too significant to throw away, but not important enough to need. But this box contained nothing of the sort. It held something of incredible importance to May. It held Memories. A dozen or so miscellaneous items filled the box, each with their own significance. May reached in and pulled out a red scarf. She gripped it tightly, remembering how she came to have it.

It had been a bad day. She had gotten so overwhelmed with all her high level classes and extracurricular activities that she had forgotten to study for her Calculus exam. That Friday, when she got her grade back and saw that she got a 72, she panicked. She didn't know what to do. She couldn't go home and face her parents after doing so poorly on such an important exam. It was 20 percent of her grade. She knew what would happen when she told her parents. They would look at her worriedly, wondering if she was falling behind or falling in with the wrong crowd. They would make more rules, pay more attention to her. *Steal what little freedom she had.*

No, May couldn't let that happen. She couldn't go home until she had a plan. So, instead of getting on the bus she messaged her mom saying that a last minute debate meeting had been called and she needed to be there. From school May walked about a mile and a half to the nearest bus stop before getting on and riding to the mall. She just needed time to clear her head. She walked around the mall before entering a store with cute, trendy clothes. She browsed around for a while before finding a pretty red flowery scarf. She looked around the store quickly to make sure no one was looking before ripping the tag off and shoving it into her backpack. It was exhilarating. She felt a wave of energy rush over her as if she were doing something dangerous. No one expected her to be capable of something like this and it made her feel good. It made her feel free. She then went back to walking around for a few more minutes before sighing loudly and hurrying out the door. She felt powerful as she made her escape. She hadn't been caught. She felt almost untouchable, as if she was free to do anything and there would never be any consequences. She caught a bus back to the bus stop and made her way back from school, arriving just a few minutes before her mom. May was lucky. Soccer practice had been canceled earlier in the week due to rain and had been rescheduled for Friday. That meant that as her mom pulled up other students were piling into cars to head home.

As May got into the car her mom smiled at her and she inwardly cringed. She just needed to get it over with.

"We got our calculus exam scores back today."

"Oh, that's wonderful honey. We'll have pizza tonight to celebrate," her mom replied brightly.

May froze. She couldn't do it.

"That sounds wonderful mom."

When they got home May went straight to her room. She rummaged around in her closet before pulling out a box of antique dolls from her grandma. She dumped the dolls out on the floor before rushing over to her bed and grabbing her bag along the way. She pulled out the scarf, running her fingers over the soft silk fabric before placing it gently into the box. That was the first time she'd done something like that, but it wouldn't be the last.

***

May placed the scarf back in the box and pulled out a different object. It was a small tube of sparkly pink strawberry flavored lip gloss. Back in her sophomore year of highschool all the girls were wearing this lipgloss. If you weren't, you were practically deemed a social outcast. May had been begging her mom for almost two weeks, but the answer was always a resounding no. Her mom's reasoning was always, "You're too young to be wearing makeup." May had stormed off to her room before shutting the door softly. She needed a solution.

The next day was Saturday and May was set to go winter clothes shopping with her mother. While her mother was searching through winter coats May slipped away to the makeup aisle. That's when she saw the lip gloss. She thought it must be fate. May hadn't done anything like this since the scarf from her freshman year. She didn't know what came over her, only that she *had* to have that lipgloss. She quickly pocketed the small tube and tugged her shirt down a little to better hide it before hurrying back to her mom. As they were waiting in line at the check out, May noticed the security scanners at the doors of the store. Her heart stopped as white hot fear flashed through her. She panicked to come up with a solution, any solution. She couldn't take it out of her pocket without any of the many shoppers and employees around her seeing her. She could tell her mom she's going to the bathroom! That's it!

"Would you like a receipt," the cashier asked, snapping May out of her thoughts. She hadn't even noticed them moving up in line.

"Yes, thank you," May's mother replied, taking the receipt and turning to May. "Are you ready to go dear?"

"Actually, would it be okay if I used the bathroom first?" May said, sure she was in the clear.

"Are you able to hold it? We're only a few minutes from home and we need to get home so I can start on dinner."

"O-okay," May said unsteadily, thinking that if she argued her mother would see her panic and unease and know what she had done. As they headed towards the doors, May held her breath, praying that if she didn't get caught she'd never do it again. Scenes played out in her head. Her being tackled by police officers, handcuffed and jailed, her mom sobbing and blaming herself for everything. Wondering where she went wrong as a mother. Did she not love her daughter enough?

Then all of the sudden they were through the doors. No alarms, no police sirens. Just the sounds of her erratic heartbeat and her blood rushing in her ears. She hadn't been caught. She felt free, liberated. That Monday as she walked into school with her head held high she noted all the girls wearing lipgloss. A girl from her English class came up to her asking loudly, "Why aren't you wearing any lipgloss? Did you forget yours at home or something? You can use mine if you want but you better not have herpes or something."

May just smiled and replied, "No thanks, I'm too young to wear makeup."

"If you say so," the girl said before notice someone else she knew and rushed over to them.

***

Placing the tube of lipgloss back in the box, May wondered how she hadn't gotten caught. Maybe the security scanners were broken, or maybe they never worked in the first place. May shook her head. It was all in the past, all that mattered is that no one knew but her. Despite what May promised herself, it did happen again, many times. After a bad grade, losing a debate, her dad missed her award ceremony because had to work late *again.* It continued to happen for many years, up until the day her parents got divorced and she realized the perfect idols she worked so hard everyday to be like and to please, were never that perfect anyways.

May locked the box, sliding it under her bed. Once again putting away the adrenaline filled days of her youth. The days where she felt truly free, like she could do anything. The days where stealing something as insignificant as a tube of lipstick felt like the biggest deal in the world. While all the effort she put in, all the hard work and joyless days had cost her so much, the feeling of taking the objects had made her free.

But that's not who she was anymore. Now she goes to work at the nursing home cleaning bedpans and begging senior citizens to take their medicine. Each day is more arduous than the last. Some days aren't so bad. She'll come home and make herself dinner and watch tv. Some days, she'll be so tired that she barely has energy to heat up a frozen meal before falling asleep on the couch. On her worst days, that's when she goes to the box. She sits there and relives the irrational actions and the excitement of her former years. That is, before she remembers that those days are far behind her. Still she has to wonder, if she did it again, would she get caught?

Miles of Solace
Jarely Rebollar

I gripped the steering wheel until my knuckles turned white, the hum of the engine a low growl against the silence that filled the car. The fight with Michael was still a raw wound, words flung like daggers still echoing in my mind. I didn't know where the direction north would take me, only that it was away from the pain, away from our apartment that now felt too small and filled with too many memories.

I could barely remember what was said at the beginning of the fight. I only remember being upset by how much time he was spending out so late at night. Michael said he'd stay out late for a work project but came stumbling back into the apartment smelling like pure alcohol. I remembered we started to argue, I was tired of him coming home so late and drinking himself half to death, and Michael was yelling at me to stop controlling his life. That's when the whole reason why he was going out so late recently came out. He's been fucking my younger sister, Liliana. My sister who just turned eighteen. *Eighteen.* Me and Michael were well into our late thirties, and he's been fucking a barely legal adult. I wasn't even upset that he'd been cheating, well I was, but it was more the fact that he had been around with Liliana for so long that he could easily take advantage of her. Now here I was, driving wherever north would take me.

The dashboard clock glowed 3:17 A.M.; the world outside was a blur of shadow and silver moonlight. Every mile put between me and Michael was a salve, yet the further I went, the more my emotional shock cooled, leaving a hollow sadness in its wake. The road stretched endlessly ahead, the darkness pressing in as if it could swallow me whole.

The only sound was the steady thrum of the tires on the pavement, a rhythm that matched the pounding of my heart. I passed a sign that read 'Northwood 50 miles,' a town name I didn't even recognize. But it didn't matter. North was not a destination; it was a direction, a way to move forward when everything inside me screamed to go back, to undo the last few hours, and to forget what Michael did. To just pretend nothing ever happened.

I should blame everything on Michael, but I was more upset with myself for not protecting her from him. Our parents always worked and could barely be home with us, so it was just me raising her. I was so blinded by how much I loved Michael that I never questioned how much differently he would behave around her, always buying her some sort of gift, taking her on some fun trip, and how he'd always tell me how she's growing into such a fine young lady. I really did believe that he was just a great guy who didn't mind how I was basically a mom to my sister. He's been taking advantage of her for that long, and I didn't even know. I just wish that I could reverse everything.

But life didn't come with a reverse gear, and as the miles accumulated, the first hints of dawn began to touch the sky, the darkness receding inch by inch. I realized the night would end, and the sun would rise, whether I was ready to face it or not. The road ahead was uncertain, unwritten, and maybe, just maybe, that was exactly what I needed.

Lullaby: The Golden Apples of the Sun
William Rowley

Despite the blur of everything else, her face was clear. She was all that mattered anyway. That said, I could still tell we were at a park, for she stood under that same gazebo as before—adorned by the radiating strings of warm white Christmas lights that added a beauty that almost rivaled her own. Almost, but not quite. A layer of simple brick beneath my feet seemed to lead me to where she stood beneath her little spotlight, and if I strained my eyes hard enough and observed my left and my right, I could see that no other visitors joined me in the luxury of taking in the sight of her—not on the benches to the left or beneath the massive oak tree to the right. In seeing me look around, she'd smile and begin to beckon me closer, words which echoed both literally and figuratively in my head. It was my name, Issac, she called, and she wanted me to come closer. And so I did, one foot before the other following the pattern of brick until I was almost close enough to touch her. My hand reached for her cheek—her hair thick, brown, and flowing like a horse's mane in the wind, but in a blink...she was gone. Her voice, music to my ears, replaced by the annoying blare of my phone's alarm. The view of her face traded for that of my dusty ceiling. Her soft cheek stolen in favor of that of my own rough and stubbled beard. It was morning.

Against my will, I pull myself out of bed and begin my boring daily routine. A shower, taking vitamins, trimming my sloppy facial-hair and dragging a comb through the thinned-out hair on the top of my head, not in that exact order—but as I do so, my mind begins to wander.

I...had that dream again...

Must be a hundred times now. A hundred heartbreaks. A hundred times I've had to wake up and face reality. And I do somehow.

But it's been more than a hundred times that I've had to wake up here alone.

I keep a chair for you near my dining table—it waits for the day you come into my life. I've even got two more to spare for any kids we decide to bring into this world. You could even be my wife.

But where are you? Are you only in my dreams? Perhaps you're the bashful type, and I must come find you first.

There is this idea of a dream girl. But my dream will come true with you.

I eventually join reality again once the list of mindless activities run their course, and my hand lands on the cool, dented metal of my front door's knob. Destination: coffee.

I wouldn't say I have a bad life. For example, my favorite coffee shop is merely two blocks away! How lucky can a man get?

No, but seriously, I suppose life has just kind of passed me by. I've grown comfortable, and it took me until it was damn-near too late to realize that. I see others my age already settled down with jobs, and lives, and wives they all love, and although I don't hate my simple life, and I don't hate working at the plant, I do hate the lack of a wife. I guess I could be like James, my coworker. His wife died last year, and they were only married for six.

Was it Poe or...Tennyson? It was Tennyson. "'Tis better to have loved and lost..." I guess.

The coffee shop was decently crowded, but not enough to disrupt my thoughts. Couples, students studying, and some old ladies gossiping about who knows what. It makes me wonder what kind of stuff we would talk about. Do you even like coffee? What a deal-breaker that would be if you didn't—this place has become a daily tradition for me on my off days. Minutes pass like seconds here each visit, and I almost feel at peace until your image pops back into mind. Haunting me. Taunting me. Today, I cannot relax. Today, I have somewhere to be. I brush my thumb across the embroidered "WAKE UP" on my hot cup before I down the straight-black coffee, and I am once again heading towards a door: the exit.

At the end of this same street, two blocks from where I live, is a mall. I remember when it was first erected some twenty-odd years ago. It was the most happening place in town, but now it stands the definition of pitiful and rundown. Ownership has changed many times over the years, with each promising to renovate the old, tired building into something of substance. Oh, don't let my harsh criticism fool you, though. Inside that decayed old building is the best bookstore in town, and my second destination of the day. Everything from the latest releases to coloring books to the complete works of Oscar Wilde—from comics to textbooks, poem compilations and bibles—this place has something for every reader, truly. Today only, I pass by the fiction shelves and head towards the section on spirituality and religion.

I have done some light research in the past on dreams and their meanings. This is exactly what led me to start writing about you. A dream journal, it's called. Pages and pages and pages filled with our love story. But I need more than that now.

I feel my brain start shifting to thoughts of you again, like something squeezing my skull from the inside-out. It wasn't until my eyes spotted the book my finger had been searching for, and I am interrupted by another's voice—not mine or yours, but a separate girl beside me, that causes this painful harping to cease.

"Sorry!" She squeaked in a soft tone as if to not disrupt the quiet vibe, all while recoiling a hand I seemed to have accidentally groped upon finding my book of choice. It was like some perfectly scripted meet-cute.

"1,000 Common Dreams Interpreted?" she commented. "I would not have marked you as the type. I love dreams, though! They're so fascinating, right?"

I couldn't say how long she went on after this, as I stopped paying attention to her quickly and never offered her a reply outside of a returned apology. She sure seemed invested in talking to me though, but I couldn't distract myself from you. From us. And no other could come between us. I had to get out of here and find you.

Frantically now, I purchase my book and leave. I can read and walk, so I do that and learn the significance of parks and dreams. It says here "You will soon have a fresh start in life." It also says some stuff about longing for a break from reality, and that I will hear good news from a sister, but I don't have a sister and that stuff didn't really pertain to me, so I paid it no mind. I needed to head to my final destination. Happiness. End game. The park where I will see you in flesh for the very first time: Celebration Park. A few miles from here.

I'm disgusting and sweaty now, but this must be it. The gazebo, the brick, the tree, I saw it all. I wouldn't let the fact that no one else seemed to be here ruin my spirits so quickly. There was that bench, and I could sit there and wait if needed. So, I do that, and minutes slowly torture me until...you are there. Or at least I think it is you. A girl, at the very least, sits right beneath your lights. Her hair is blonde, not brown, and she seems a little younger, and a little short-er, but...the parallels are uncanny outside of that, although I didn't get a good look at her face. All signs lead to this being my moment, that today would be the day!

Just like the dream, I stand to look down at my feet and follow the brick, but only this time I am interrupted early. Not by my alarm clock, but by another man cutting me off in a jog and perching him-self beside you. Or at least I think it was you. The two share a quick kiss, and what they start to talk about I do not know. At this point, the whole day had started to make me feel all too tired.

"I think I'll head back home now." I whisper to no one but myself.

P.O. Box: St. Nick
William Rowley

"It's been raining for three fucking days straight." That's what Paul said—I remember because that's a bad word.

The middle-aged man wearing a peacoat and a beer belly stood staring out the glass front door of the post office. It was too bad like three feet of snow had barricaded him and everyone inside from exiting, but that didn't stop him from trying the door every hour or so. His anger kept him from seeing the good news, though: It wasn't *raining* for three days straight, it had been snowing for two, and *now* it was raining. Temperatures had risen some, the snowfall had relaxed, and we shouldn't be getting any more snow until after Christmas. I thought rain would make the streets all slippery and stuff, but my grandpa says the warmer weather means the rain will fall at a higher temperature than the snow sits in, and that will help melt the snow. I'm not sure who's right, though—Paul, my grandpa-pa, or me.

At his outburst, my Mommy, who was at my right, gave me a little nudge and smiled and tried not to laugh too loud at angry Paul. To my left, my grandpa-pa, who had his head down in relaxation, simply shook his head 'no' to show some silent dissatisfaction with Paul's apparent anger problems. We all sat occupying three of the five seats lined up in the waiting room of the office. To my grandpa's right sat Julie. She was a girl about ten years older than me, and to *her* right was Nancy, a sweet old lady even older than my grandpa-pa! Jeffery was also here, but he worked here and kept himself busy gathering some stuff behind the counter.

So, in total you had:

My mommy.
My grandpa-pa.
Jeffrey, the office worker.
Julie, the teenage girl.
Nancy, the lady even older than my grandpa-pa.
And the mad man Paul.

Oh, and I should probably go back and say it's not like we have been stuck inside this place for three days. I'm not sure we'd last that long. See, me and my mommy and my grandpa-pa drove here yesterday to drop off some extra late, extra last minute Christmas gifts for family that live out of state. That was the 20th of December. The snow was falling then, and we thought we would beat the bad weather, but it was basically only sleeting when we left and...well, I guess we were wrong, so we've been stuck here since yesterday evening. That's when we all went around introducing ourselves.

Everyone liked Jeffery from the start. See, while everyone was figuring out how we were going to make the morning, Jeffery had prepared hot chocolate for everyone—saving himself for last. I never did ask Jeffery how old he was, but I'd guess around forty. Jeffery was the friendliest, and the tallest, and the skinniest, and he did his best to make everyone feel more comfy-cozy. It was his idea for us all to sit in a circle and tell our hopes for both Christmas gifts, and for the new year. He even made a little envelope with our names on it, and said he knew Santa's address. He said he'd send all our letters together!

Nancy, the really really old lady? She went first because she loved the idea Jeffery came up with. She went on to say how her life had been hard since she lost her husband, and the idea of getting to talk to a bunch of people had her giddy, but I don't know that word. Still, mixed in with the stories she told of Christmases of the past, she reminded everyone that help would be on the way soon.

"This year, Santa, I just want to make it another year." Wrote Nancy

Paul was checking the door again when Nancy passed the envelope to Julie. Julie's got a boyfriend. He lives far, far away she said, though. I think in Florida? Julie said they met online and started dating, and that she was here to send off his Christmas box. I could tell it was really important to her, whatever it was, because instead of giving her box to Jeffery she kept it sitting in her lap the whole time we were here waiting. Me and Julie spent most of yesterday talking about our classes, and boys, and our favorite Christmas food. I heard my Mom thank her for "keeping me distracted" while the adults figured out a gameplan for the night.

"I want things to work out between us" is what she wrote. I saw it on accident.

Granpa-pa took the letter from Julie and paused for a moment. He did that thing he does with every pen that touches his hands where he taps it to his chin, then his lips, and it's like it's slowly getting closer to being in his mouth until he's chewing on the end of it. It's SO gross! But still, that's Grandpa-pa and I love him and his nasty pen-nibbling. I lost track of just how long he was thinking for because I was staring at the way he gnawed on that pen for so long. Once he was passing the letter to Mommy, the cap didn't even fit the end of the pen anymore. I'm sorry, Santa! I don't mean to be rude, it's just! It's all slobbery, okay?

"I hope the turkey and dressing is cooked better than last year, and all that dark meat is saved for me." That's what he wished for. I saw because it was supposed to be my turn next, but Paul rejoined our circle then, and I let him go before me.

162

I didn't expect Paul to write anything. I expected Paul to be on the naughty list. Paul may have been a moody man, but he wasn't a bad man. I don't think he was used to letting out his feelings because he wrote so much that Jeffery had to get another sheet of paper just for me and my Mommy to have room too. I know I probably shouldn't look at what everyone else was writing, but I had to! Sorry! Paul was kinda like Nancy because he wasn't married anymore neither, but Paul's wife didn't pass away like Nancy's husband did. Paul lost his job over the Spring, and his wife over the Summer. She left him for another man and took their daughter with her. The court thought a woman with a job would be a better guardian than a man without one. Paul had a lot to ask Santa, but I don't think Paul was really writing to him.

"If I can't have you back, then at least let me see my daughter." That's how his letter ended.

Mommy went next. Mommy read Paul's writing too, I could tell. She kept looking up at him, then back to her paper, then back to him, and back to her paper. She watched even as he went back to the front door to watch the rain fall over the snow. I think Mommy likes Paul now, or feels bad for him, because she looks at him the same way Julie said she looks at her boyfriend when she does get to see him, or the way Nancy said she stared in the eyes of her former husband when she was telling stories of their marriage. I don't think she wanted anyone to know how she really felt about Paul, though, because she scribbled through a lot of her words and didn't write lots like most others.

"I hope everyone's packages make it in time. It'll take a miracle for that."

Finally, it was my turn. At first I was going to write how I really, *really* hope I can get a puppy this year! I'm six-going-on-seven now and I can handle the responsibility, but...I'm not going to ask for that. I've asked for that for forever, so I think everyone knows I want that. Instead, I decided I'd make mine brief too. I just hope everyone's wishes come true times a hundred-million, and that next years Christmas is better than this years', and that we don't get stuck anywhere!

When I stuffed the envelope all nice together and handed it back to Jeffery, he told me the city workers would be here soon to scrape the snow away. We'd finally be able to leave, but I'm going to miss everyone here...even Paul.

163

SEVEN DAYS, SEVEN-HUNDRED DOLLARS
William Rowley

Callie needed cash. *Fast* cash.

Being a broke college student was a day-to-day challenge. It's the equivalent of waking up every day and being slapped in the face. By the time you hit your Junior year, it's like the slap turns into being kidnapped. Every day, you're kidnapped. Held against your will. Years of the best years of your life stolen from you to pursue a degree you really weren't as passionate about as your parents were. That's Callie's problem. Her solution, though, might be that new ad she saw on Indeed.

"SEVEN DAYS, SEVEN-HUNDRED DOLLARS"

Too good to be true? House-sitting can't be that hard, she told herself. You just sit...in a house. She does that every day, so the Millers' mansion should just be more house to sit in. That's all.

Day one just proved her assumptions. A single piece of paper on the marble kitchen counter sloppily jotted down her instructions. She had the freedom to use the pool, the golf-course, the home theatre, the kitchen, the library—nothing was off limits. Nothing but the room on the third floor at the far end. Callie happily took the big master bedroom on the first floor for herself, and figured she wouldn't even go to the third floor *ever*, so it all seemed easy enough. The night was spent comfortably sleeping in the array of positions a King sized bed allotted for.

Day two provided some challenge. The Millers' were an older couple, in their late 70's, and that would explain why the internet was awful. Dead zones were all over the house, and even Callie's 5G wouldn't work. She was a young girl left smartphone-less.

Callie wasn't really a reader, so the library held little interest to her. Sure, she skimmed the room out of sheer boredom and picked up a few books; namely Mary Shelley's *Frankenstein*, but when she saw it wasn't written at a middle-school reading level she quickly put it down next to a title labeled *Strange Case of Dr. Jekyll and Mr. Hyde*. Even a middle-schooler would have known *Shelley* comes before *Stevenson* in an alphabetically organized shelf. Still, without her phone or a book to read, she somehow survived the night.

Day three was when Callie left the first floor for the first time. The home theatre was there on the second, and she looked at the ninety-eight-inch screen as her savior. All hope was shattered swiftly when she saw the projector *didn't* use Netflix. Her choices had to be hand-selected, and with movies like *Re-animator*, *The Human Centipede*, and *Martyrs* her only options, she knew she couldn't stomach to watch any of the Millers' movies. By the end of day three, she was starting to see the old Millers' in a different light.

Day four, she was past the halfway point of those seven nights. Nothing had gone wrong, except the little annoyances here and there, but she was still being paid to live in a mansion. Really, it wasn't a bad gig. The little voice in her head had started tempting her to check out the third floor, though. The steps of the spiraling staircase grew worse for wear the closer she got to reaching her destination; a sign that the Millers' frequented this floor the most. Impressive for an elderly couple, she thought. On this floor were seven rooms; three on the left side of the hall, three on the right, and one at the end. Callie entered them in order, from left to right, and the time she spent in each decreased during her exploration, for she only found what seemed to be guest bedrooms in each one. Rooms reserved for extended family? The 8x10 framed photos of girls along the walls of each respective room would back that suspicion. But if so, why did the Millers' reserve the most rundown, subpar rooms in the mansion for family? Furthermore, the Millers sure seemed to have a lot of granddaughters. Bored of this, Callie wouldn't even bother with the last room. She wasn't supposed to go in there anyway, and figured it was more of the same. She was fine respecting those wishes and returned to the first floor.

One hour into day five, in the middle of the night, Callie's curiosity got the best of her. Fueled by paranoia, she fumbled out of bed and crept up the staircase until she was staring down the hallway of the third floor—all while the framed girls along said hall stared at her. Before turning the hallway lights on, she noticed a green glow coming from beneath the last room. The room she *hadn't* entered—so she knew she did *not* just forget to turn those lights off. She moved inward and reached for the metal handle which only greeted her with coldness, then pushed her way inside—breaking the one rule the Millers' laid out.

Old Mr. Miller was there to greet her, dressed in a large white coat and glasses too large for his old, weathered face.

"You just couldn't follow the rules, could you?" he croaked, and raised a syringe.

Callie started for the door, but little Mrs. Miller was there, hunchback and all, pistol at the ready if Callie didn't give her body willingly to the table in front of Mr. Miller.

On day six, Callie wasn't breathing.

On day seven, Callie, in multiple pieces, was completely stiff.

On day eight, Callie made the news.

On day nine, the Millers' had Callie's photo along the hallway of the third floor.

On day ten, a new ad was posted on Indeed.

"EIGHT DAYS, EIGHT-HUNDRED DOLLARS"

Scholarly Essays

Self-Taught Versus Trained: Virtuosity in Heavy Metal

Robyn Gerry

Virtuosity, quintessentially established in jazz and classical, does not stop there. From 1950 to 1960, heavy metal guitarists Van Halen, Malstreem, Randy Rhodes, and Hendrix started to form a type of virtuosity, named guitar virtuosity, that other heavy metal guitarists would want to achieve. Fast riffs, technical licks, and advanced ornamentation on solos were the guitar techniques that were the base requirements to become a guitar virtuoso. The one thing they had in common was that they all had music theory backgrounds, either classically trained on the guitar or piano. The representation of their music training is through the composition of their music referencing classical pieces to show people that heavy metal was an actual music genre and not noise. Now not all heavy metal guitarists are trained musicians. You have George Lynch, Matt Heafy, and Michael Schenker, who were all self-taught guitarists and did not know any music theory, yet still obtained the label of a guitar virtuoso from a unique style. A guitar virtuoso is a musician with skilled ability, technique, or personal style. This definition of virtuosity and having guitarists that are trained or self-taught brings up a question. Is there a difference in virtuosity between trained guitarists versus self-taught guitarists?[1]

While musical scholars and historians assert different meanings to "virtuosity," there are aspects of the concept within guitar repertoire that are evolving. Historian Kevin Erbert tries to separate the meaning of self-taught and trained to achieve a virtuoso. He explains that for a virtuoso, the musicians need to understand what they are accomplishing, putting self-taught musicians lower on the scale. Other historians believe there is a small middle area of being self-taught and trained, but still believe music theory is key. Historian Lucy Green explains that self-taught guitarists are at the same virtuosity level as trained musicians, which is different from Ebert's reasoning because he believes there is no such thing as a self-taught guitarist. Her reasoning is later in their career they have some sort of formal training, which she considers "bi-musical" meaning a musician is taught formally and informally. Still, these two historians show that music theory is a key to becoming a virtuoso as the musician needs to know what they are doing, which is where historian Lars Lilliestam's, meaning shows a unique perspective. Lilliestam's view on virtuosity is that self-taught guitarist has the same level of skill as trained guitarists. Even though self-taught guitarists might not understand what they are playing because they do not have music theory training, they develop their own personal style, which is explained in the definition of guitar virtuosity. Combining their personal style with how they were trained shows a different level of virtuosity in her view. A type of virtuosity unique to their own way of playing the guitar and where it shows in their music. She does explain the use of formal training and it is benefits to musicians but does not say that it's the only way to become a true heavy metal virtuoso. With all the viewpoints of historians, they all bring up one question to achieve for a virtuoso that has been a debate in the heavy metal world. Does music theory play a key role in guitar virtuosity? A guitar virtuoso does not have to be trained in guitar technique; a self-taught guitarist at the virtuoso level is also considered a virtuoso. Unlike formally trained guitarists, a self-taught guitarist does not need to have the smallest understanding of music theory, they have a personal style.[2]

Virtuosity in heavy metal took time for people to see that heavy metal can be virtuosic, through the guitar players. There was still the stigma that heavy metal was not real music. People believed that heavy metal music was just a bunch of noise with no meaning. Classical music, jazz, and blues were considered real music, which are the foundation genres of heavy metal music. Before Van Halen or Randy Rhodes, guitar virtuosos were from progressive rock or the classical genres of music like Glenn Buxton. When Randy Rhodes, Van Halen, Steve Vai, and Jimi Hendrix became known, their use of adopting previous guitar virtuosos to their own started to see guitarists in the heavy metal world become more well-known and then placed the virtuoso tag. Heavy metal fans saw virtuosos as people who could play fast, but digging deeper into how a musician becomes a virtuoso there has been a split in the heavy metal genre, a debate called feeling versus theory.[3]

The debate of feeling versus theory stems from the difference in virtuosity between self-taught and trained metal guitarists. The theory side focuses on trained musicians and the need for music theory to become a virtuoso. Having the knowledge of music theory shows an understanding of what a musician is playing and how a certain piece or genre of music should be performed. This idea is where trained musicians are categorized in. This idea compares to a painter who sees colors. Color is to a painter as music theory is to a trained musician. Having the foundation of music, a musician will be able to understand their instrument and know how to play music. When discussing the feeling aspect, the main concept is emotion. Going back to the example of a painter, this idea describes abstract art. A painter does not need to understand color and mix certain colors to obtain a good work of art. A painter just like a metal guitarist can use emotion to portray what they are feeling in that moment.

The interesting statistical data is that fifty-three percent of metal guitarists are self-taught and only nineteen percent of metal guitarists are trained musicians. With this statistical data, there should not be an issue with virtuosity in heavy metal, but there still is. Besides the issue of musicians should know music theory there is music terminology that has been incorrectly used, which has caused a part of the split in the debate.[4]

Even with this new virtuosity in heavy metal, over time people started to see the "importance" of music theory and how it will help metal guitarists, which caused other music terminology to be used incorrectly to explain what a virtuoso is. The two main terms are musicality and the classical version of virtuosity. The definition of musicality is musical talent. Self-taught or trained every musician has musical talent. Musicians have musical talent when they have played for a year or twenty years, musicians have musicality. Self-taught guitarists have been "classified" as having musicality, but not having virtuosity. The classical definition of virtuosity is a great skill in music. To this day, heavy metal historians still believe that music theory is the way to achieve virtuosity rather than a personal style.[5]

Being a trained musician can stem from having formal lessons to having a degree in music. After heavy metal became a huge music genre, music schools began adding guitar classes and music theory majors because everyone wanted to learn guitar and become a heavy metal guitarist. One example is the Berklee School of Music which has created a huge name as one of the best music schools in the modern day, but for heavy metal one of the first heavy metal guitarists to have a degree in music is Steve Vai. Steve Vai did not just go to Berklee to get guitar techniques; he also went to obtain music theory training by reading music. "When I went to Berklee, I had all this technique and skill, but there was so much that I needed to learn as far as reading and music theory. In fact, all the stuff I learned, I used right away in early songwriting.[6]

Steve Vai was born in 1960 and had a different upbringing in the music world. His parents were not musicians but were avid fans of musicals. His start to instrumental music started to develop when he was four years old when he sat down at a piano and was starting to match notes on each register. "When seeing notes on a paper, he then recognized this relation and henceforth got highly fascinated by drawing scores himself." With his fascination and talent for understanding the basics of music, he then started taking music, but it was not on the guitar or piano. It was on the accordion. The accordion has three mechanisms that after you break each one of them down show what a guitar does, melodies, and harmonies. Taking accordion lessons helped Vai learn how to blend music with different instruments. In high school, he believed that he obtains more music theory through being in an orchestra. The curriculum in an orchestra or a band in high school requires students to learn or already know music theory. With his knowledge from high school and lessons, he wanted something more than just high school music theory, this is where Berklee becomes Vai's stepping stone. Steve Vai got a degree in music theory from Berklee and it was what he called the missing piece he needed to have a better music composition and understanding in technique.[7]

After seeing a world-renowned metal guitarist get a degree in music theory from a university, universities started to promote and make metal guitar degrees for people to get a degree in music and become a true heavy metal guitarist. People would see universities promoting these degrees with the quote, "You want to be a heavy metal guitarist, all you need to do is get a degree." Ten years later, that eventually died down, as most people did not want to go get a four-year degree to become a heavy metal guitarist because the profession was still looked down upon. It is rare to find a heavy metal guitarist with a degree in music theory like Steve Vai, and this is where another form of trained guitarist starts to show. Guitarists like Randy Rhodes and Eddie Van Halen who have taken formal music theory and technique classes are the main form of trained guitarists.[8]

Two of the most well-known and influential trained guitarists during the start of heavy metal are Randy Rhoads and Eddie Van Halen, who were rival virtuosos during their time. They are not rivals because one is trained and the other is self-taught. Randy Rhoads and Eddie Van Halen both grew up in musical families and both were trained in guitar or piano. What made them rivals was how they played guitar and how they performed riffs, and how their knowledge of music theory and training helped start the type of riffs and other technical guitar techniques to obtain the label of a virtuoso. Every time one guitarist performed a new technique on stage, another guitarist wanted to do it ten times better.[9]

Randy Rhodes was born in 1956 to a musical family. His mother and father were both music teachers, with his mother being one of the teachers at the well-known music school Musonia Music. This music school was where Randy Rhodes was trained in acoustic guitar, electric guitar, and music theory. During his early life, his mother put him in the orchestra as the pianist in the music school to help him learn how to blend different instruments together into a song. He also had two other mentors Bonnie Shiekmim and Scott Shelly who helped him with both acoustic and electric guitar. Shiekmim teaches Rhoads different rhythms, but also chord harmony, which is common in classical guitar compositions such as Paganini. This mentor of Randy Rhoads provided the theory aspect of Rhoads's music career using different harmonies and showing what different harmonies can show in a piece when using different techniques. He studied under Scott Shelly who taught him electric guitar where Rhoads started to excel with riffs, licks, and heavy ornamentation. It started with chords to harmonic chords, to licks, riffs, and finally the I-IV-V chord progression. The fluidity and Rhoads, fast progression, and understanding of the chord progressions and advanced guitar techniques caused Shelly to tell his mother that there is no longer anything to teach him. With no one able to teach him because of how far he progressed, Rhoads starts to develop his personal style with what he had learned in his earlier life which is shown when he was in his band Quiet Riot. This is a perfect example of how both trained and self-taught musicians develop their own personal style. Randy Rhoads and his rival, Eddie Van Halen focused more on the speed of classical pieces like Paganini and ornamentation like Bach to compose their music.[10]

Eddie Van Halen was born in 1955 in The Netherlands also to a musical family such as Randy Rhodes. Van Halen's father was a concert saxophonist and clarinet. After Van Halen and his family moved from Holland to America, he started to learn piano and trained in music theory. Van Halen learned music theory and technical goals from the piano, then transfers them to the guitar. Van Halen said in an interview saying he is a trained musician and gives an explanation. "Did you take formal lessons? Sure. Learn to read? Oh, yeah! Definitely. I slightly know how to read for the guitar, because I know notes. But like if I see an A or an E, I do not know which one it is in relation to the piano. But piano, yeah, I played for a long time. Got all my musical theory and stuff like that from playing piano. We used to have this old Russian teacher that was a super concert pianist, and that is what our parents wanted us to be, was concert pianists." Even though Van Halen did not have guitar lessons like Randy Rhoads, his training was from his large knowledge of music theory and being able to transpose piano to guitar. This interview shows that Van Halen has music theory knowledge from being trained on the piano and thus helping him with guitar. If the "true" definition of virtuosity is having someone formally trained in music theory be the reason they are a virtuoso, Van Halen and Randy Rhodes are two perfect examples of what historians consider true virtuosos. These three trained musicians, even though they did not all come from the same upbringing and each did not follow the same aspect of what lessons they had to gain in theory and technique, their music has something in common. It has a set structure.[11]

Listening to trained guitarists' music, people can recognize there is a set structure of how the music sounds. Going back to heavy metal music using classical, jazz, and blues to show that metal music is not sound, it is just noise, it was also how guitarists like Randy Rhoads composed music. The focus was on classical music more in the Baroque era where the guitar techniques were displayed in the music composed by Bach and other composers. Baroque music like Bach had introduced a type of ornamentation that other composers saw as wild, the same with Paganini and the speed his music was able to achieve. The use of classical work in metal music created a structure for how the music was played, and depending on which guitarists, they would add their own personal style to make it unique to themselves, but also the band they were in. They understand that the structure of classical music worked during the baroque era and adding the techniques from heavy metal with the arpeggios and harmonies from classical music made music that people believed was not just noise.[12]

With all three of these musicians' people can understand that music theory, lessons, and possibly a higher degree in music are how you can get to the label of virtuoso fast, and shows people how well-known they are versed in music knowledge. This understanding and upbringing may be correct but excludes musicians who never had this upbringing or music theory understanding, i.e., self-taught guitarists.

Self-taught guitarists or musicians are people having knowledge or skills acquired by their own dedication without formal instruction. They use intuition or feeling of the music to create their own personal style. This intuition and personal style are what makes self-taught guitarists virtuoso because they see music differently. Musicians can learn music theory on their own, but some heavy metal guitarists do not believe that music theory is what makes guitarists virtuosos. Some might believe that if they had learned music theory before it would have made them a better guitarist, but it would ruin other aspects that made their playing unique. Believe it or not, a good chunk of heavy metal guitarists is self-taught. Examples include George Lynch, Matt Heafy, and Brix Vixen, yet historians still are debating if self-taught guitarists are true virtuosos because they do not follow the usually structured lessons and music theory knowledge. With the continuing debate of feeling versus theory, self-taught guitarists still have trouble figuring out if they will be accepted into the virtuosity world which should not be an issue since there are more self-taught guitarists than trained guitarists in heavy metal.[13]

The first self-taught guitarist that will be analyzed in the paper has a unique upbringing in music. Matt Heafy was born in 1986. He learned a tenor saxophone until he started teaching himself how to play the guitar around age 11. Since Heafy had learned an instrument, he is a trained musician, but that is incorrect. If a trained musician is a musician that knows music theory and Matt Heafy is not considered a trained musician. All we know is that he learned how to read sheet music for the saxophone, but in several interviews, he states that it does not help with how he learned how to play guitar. "Self-taught for quite a bit of it did lessons on and off for maybe two or three years, but I do not know anything formal music on guitar." It seems his upbringing is like Eddie Van Halen, but what makes Heafy different from Van Halen is what instrument he learned to obtain theory. Van Halen learned classical piano where music theory is needed more than an alto sax. This area of self-taught guitarists is why historians are trying to break the meaning of what a self-taught guitarist is. Matt Heafy did learn how to read sheet music, but that does not mean he understood the vocabulary or the note to meaning. When talking about note to meaning, it is describing if a musician sees a g-major scale, they can explain what notes are in a g-major scale and where the whole and half steps are to create the correct fingering. There is another interview where Matt Heafy does specify that he is a self-taught musician going back on the fact he never had lessons, and does not have the music theory training that other formally trained guitarists get with lessons. But also brings back that he did learn how to read music on the saxophone and tried to bring any technique he learned from reading music to help him develop skills on the guitar. Since some self-taught metal guitarists learned how to play an instrument, but never understood theory or stopped lessons in their career, it shows that music theory is not for everyone. Self-taught guitarists such as Britt Lightning never understood music theory and taught themselves how to play guitar, but this shows the issue of self-taught guitarists being underrecognized, because of the lack of music theory.[14]

An unknown self-taught guitarist and unknown guitar virtuoso is a female guitarist by the name of Britt Lightning. There is not much of her early life or how she got into guitar, only that she started to play the flute, but does not explain if she ever took lessons. She ended up trading her flute in and got her guitar and started to listen to guitarists that she looked up to like Jimi Hendrix and Van Halen. This way of listening to music over and over and then playing it is how some self-taught guitarists learn. We know she is self-taught from one of the interviews she gave when talking about her new album with her band Vixen, but she also brings up her opinion of being considered a virtuoso. "I am self-taught for the most part, so my approach has mostly been shaped by the artists that influenced me when I first started playing" She sees the people that influenced her as Van Halen, and Jimi Hendrix as guitar virtuosos. The one thing the guitarists that influenced her is they all have music theory knowledge. "I don't consider myself a virtuoso because people like Eddie Van Halen, Steve Vai, Joe Satriani, Jeff Beck, and so many amazing players exist." Britt has her own personal style, which is what makes up a guitar virtuoso. She goes more into melodies, and the different types of vibratos you can get with an electric guitar instead of the normal riffs. "I really enjoy melody, especially catchy ones, so the straight-up shredding does not really get me off so much anymore as much as a great bend with great vibrato, for example. As I have been playing longer, I have also realized the importance of space, like the lack of notes, which is just as important as a note." She also explains how guitar playing is ever-changing, so there will always be more guitar virtuosos coming of age in heavy metal. "But the cool thing is that guitar and all music itself is a never-ending process; it can never be mastered. And there is no end to its extent, so everyone always has something to work on and improve upon." With this quote, Britt Lightning explains that guitar technique is evolving, explaining that musicians that are self-taught are seeing a new window of opportunity to make metal music designed from style and not from mechanics and theory. George Lynch shares a similar viewpoint on how music theory is not for everyone, but also shares through an interview that there is not always a need for mechanics and theory when it comes to metal music.[15]

George Lynch was born in 1954 with a very different upbringing than Randy Rhodes or Steve Vai but still looked up to them for inspiration. Lynch did not come from a musical family and he did not take lessons. He started playing the guitar at the age of ten and was naturally gifted, but never invested in lessons. The guitar became an outlet for Lynch as he saw his passion for playing guitar as something he could turn into his own personal style. In interviews, Lynch explains his guitar playing or how he learned as undisciplined or unnatural because he never took lessons. "That intuition, coupled with an open mind and a remarkable passion for the guitar, has seen Lynch explore a wide range of genres and build a staggering body of work as a solo artist and featured guitarist." With his intuition and passion for the guitar, he also has a different way of playing the guitar. Not by music theory and understanding how each note works on a piece, but by how the music feels and how it can be expressed if it was only a guitar and the audience is completely quiet. "There is so much to say without playing endless streams of notes.

I try to explore all the parameters of guitar music and composition. I am always aware of the value of subtlety and silence. Speed and angst have their place, but I think you should incorporate all the elements in an intelligent way." If the definition of guitar virtuosity is a musician with skilled ability, technique, or personal style George Lynch is a guitar virtuoso, and it does not matter whether he has music theory knowledge or none. Lynch has also said in interviews that music theory is not for everyone and it does not mean they are less of a guitar player than a trained one. With his own personal experience after becoming a teacher, he had to learn some theory to teach his students, but when it came to his own music or composing music, music theory could never really fit. "I think it's just a different way, they're wired differently, and that's what they need to do to get there. It's wherever you need to do to get there." No person thinks the same as another and it comes to music theory as well. If music theory helps one musician and not the other, both are still great musicians, they just have a different way of learning. "And sometimes I think I'm afraid to learn because I might spoil a good thing." Seeing what music theory started to change his style of playing when teaching showed him that it was taking away from his personal style and draining the passion, he had for playing. Music theory to some musicians is a robot following orders. Music theory takes away from personal feelings and makes playing music a slew of notes.[16]

How self-taught guitarists' virtuosity is different from trained guitarists' lack of structure. This idea of structure does stem from music theory and guitar training, but self-taught guitarists will compose or play music with feeling. Feeling is compared to abstract art; abstract art has no structure. An artist can do anything with abstract art, it can be vibrant to show happiness, or dark to show sadness or anger. It is similar when hearing metal music from self-taught guitarists. One example would be Britt Lightning playing one of her guitar solos. When listening to the guitar solo there is no definite structure in the music. Being a classically trained violinist for ten years, listening to the video there could be arpeggios or certain ornamentations to make the piece flow better. This is not what self-taught guitarists think about, they think about more what they are feeling in the moment. Another example would be a guitar solo by Neil Young that George Lynch played. There is only one note in the entire song, so theory would not be an issue, this is where feeling really comes into play. Only having one note, you can play it vibrant, or hard and heavy. With the evolution of guitar techniques and how people are learning how to play the guitar feeling is becoming the more popular way for musicians to learn rather than paying money for lessons and learning theory.[17]

With both "types" of virtuosity there is a difference in how each musician plays, and how they learned how to play the guitar. This does not mean that one type of musician is better capable to be a virtuoso or has better skill and technique on the guitar to make them a virtuoso. Both self-taught guitarists and trained guitarists both are virtuosos despite the knowledge of music theory or lessons. With any genre of music, there comes a point in time when music and technique are evolving where theory is outweighed. The feeling can overpower theory.

Endnotes

[1] Walser, Robert, (1993), 'Running With The Devil: Power, Gender, and Madness in Heavy Metal Music', Middletown: Wesleyan University Press.

[2] Ebert, Kevin. (2017) "But That Doesn't Help Me on Guitar!" Connecting Metal to Culture, pp. 163–190.; Green, Lucy (2001), How Popular Musicians Learn: A Way Ahead for Music Education, Farnham: Ashgate.; Lilliestam, Lars (1996), 'On playing by ear.' Popular Music, 15: 2, pp. 195-216.

[3] Walser, Robert, (1993), 'Running With The Devil: Power, Gender, and Madness in Heavy Metal Music', Middletown: Wesleyan University Press.

[4] Walser, Robert, (1993), 'Running With The Devil: Power, Gender, and Madness in Heavy Metal Music', Middletown: Wesleyan University Press.

[5] Merriam-Webster.com Dictionary, s.v. "musicality," accessed April 25, 2023, https://www.merriam-webster.com/dictionary/musicality; Merriam-Webster.com Dictionary, s.v. "virtuosity," accessed April 25, 2023, https://www.merriam-webster.com/dictionary/virtuosity.

[6] Petrucci, John, (2011), 'Exclusive interview with Dream Theater's John Petrucci: Why their songs are so long, music industry advice, and how he knew Mike Mangini was the'; Satriani, Joe, and Brown J., (2014), Strange Beautiful Music: A Musical Memoir, Dallas; Skolnick, Alex, (1989), 'Musicology', Guitar for the Practicing Musician, December, pp. 70-76.

[7] Custodis, Michael. "Living history: The guitar virtuoso and composer Steve Vai." In *Heavy Metal, Gender and Sexuality*, pp. 55-70. Routledge, 2016

[8] Locker, Melissa. "Earn a College Degree in Heavy Metal. Really." Time. Time, May 15, 2013. https://newsfeed.time.com/2013/05/15/earn-a-college-degree-in-heavy-metal-really/.

[9] Carew, Francis Wayne, "The Guitar Voice of Randy Rhoads" (2018). Wayne State University, Theses. 611; Obrecht, Jas, (2011), Eddie Van Halen: The Complete 1978, Interviews

[10] Carew, Francis Wayne, "The Guitar Voice of Randy Rhoads" (2018). Wayne State University, Theses. 611.

[11] Obrecht, Jas, (2011), Eddie Van Halen: The Complete 1978, Interviews; Obrecht, Jas, (2010), Eddie Van Halen: The David Lee Rotha Era

[12] Béra, Camille. (2016). Virtuosity in Heavy Metal. 10.13140/RG.2.2.19224.01287.

[13] Murimi, Esther. "What Does Is It Really Mean to Be a Self-Taught Musician?" *Merriam Music - Toronto's Top Piano Store & Music School*, 9 June 2022, https://www.merriam-music.com/school-of-music/meaning-of-self-taught-musician/.

[14] Heafy, Matt, (2011), 'An exclusive interview with Matt Heafy', Facebook, 11 March; Heafy, Matt, (2010), Gear Nerd: Guitars with Matt Heafy

[15] Daly, Andrew, (2022), 'An Interview with Britt Lightning of Vixxen'

[16] David Von Bader, (2021), "George Lynch: I Tend to be Naturally Undisciplined"; Mark McStea, (2020), "George Lynch: There's so much to say without playing endless streams of notes- I'm always aware of the values of subtlety and silence"; David Slavkovic, (2022), "George Lynch Says He Doesn't Know Much Music Theory, Explains why he doesn't need it"; Walser, Robert(1993), 'Running With The Devil: Power, Gender, and Madness in Heavy Metal Music', Middletown: Wesleyan University Press.

[17] Wethington, William. "Britt Lightning soloing on Stranglehold I was singing" December 31,2022. 0:31. https://youtu.be/9coVESbkzhc.; Gene51. "George Lynch Wicked Sensation Solo Outtakes" March 16, 2017. 9:50. https://youtu.be/DfU-JGmiX_Q.

Bibliography

Primary Sources

Daly, Andrew. 'An Interview with Britt Lightning of Vixxen.' Other. *https://vwmusicrocks.com*, October 12, 2022. https://vwmusicrocks.com/an-interview-with-britt-lightning-of-vixen-2/.

Heafy, Matt, Gear Nerd: Guitars with Matt Heafy, 2010

Heafy, Matt, 'An exclusive interview with Matt Heafy', Facebook, 2011

McStea, Mark. George Lynch: "There's so much to say without playing endless streams of notes – I'm always aware of the value of subtlety and silence." Other. *Guitarworld.com,* August 24, 2020. https://www.guitarworld.com/features/george-lynch-theres-so-much-to-say-without-playing-endless-streams-of-notes-im-always-aware-of-the-value-of-subtlety-and-silence.

Obrecht, Jas, Eddie Van Halen: The David Lee Rotha Era, 2010

Obrecht, Jas, Eddie Van Halen: The Complete 1978, Interviews, 2011

Petrucci, John, 'Exclusive interview with Dream Theater's John Petrucci: Why their songs are so long, music industry advice, and how he knew Mike Mangini was the',2011

Satriani, Joe, and Brown J., Strange Beautiful Music: A Musical Memoir, 2014

Slavkovic, David. George Lynch Says He Doesn't Know Much Music Theory, Explains Why He Doesn't Need It. Other. *www.ultimate-Guitar.com*, March 22, 2022. https://www.ultimate-guitar.com/news/general_music_news/george_lynch_says_he_doesnt_know_much_music_theory_explains_why_he_doesnt_need_it.html.

Von Bader, David. George Lynch: "I Tend to Be Naturally Undisciplined." Other. *www.premierguitar.com*, March 4, 2021. https://www.premierguitar.com/artists/george-lynch-i-tend-to-be-naturally-undisciplined.

Secondary Sources

Béra, Camille, Virtuosity in Heavy Metal. 10.13140/RG.2.2.19224.01287. 2016

Carew, Francis Wayne, "The Guitar Voice of Randy Rhoads" (2018). Wayne State University, Theses. 611.

Custodis, Michael. "Living history: The guitar virtuoso and composer Steve Vai." In *Heavy Metal, Gender and Sexuality*, pp. 55-70. Routledge, 2016.

Ebert, Kevin. "But That Doesn't Help Me on Guitar!" (2017) Connecting Metal to Culture, pp. 163–190.

Gene51. "George Lynch Wicked Sensation Solo Outtakes" March 16, 2017. 9:50. https://youtu.be/DfU-JGmiX_Q.

Green, Lucy, How Popular Musicians Learn: A Way Ahead for Music Education, Farnham: Ashgate, 2001

Lilliestam, Lars, 'On playing by ear.' Popular Music, 15: 2, pp. 195-216.1996

Locker, Melissa. "Earn a College Degree in Heavy Metal. Really." *Time*. Time, May 15, 2013. https://newsfeed.time.com/2013/05/15/earn-a-college-degree-in-heavy-metal-really/.

Merriam-Webster.com Dictionary, s.v. "musicality," accessed April 25, 2023, https://www.merriam-webster.com/dictionary/musicality

Merriam-Webster.com Dictionary, s.v. "virtuosity," accessed April 25, 2023, https://www.merriam-webster.com/dictionary/virtuosity.

Murimi, Esther. "What Does Is It Really Mean to Be a Self-Taught Musician?" *Merriam Music—Toronto's Top Piano Store & Music School*, 9 June 2022, https://www.merriammusic.com/school-of-music/meaning-of-self-taught-musician/.

Walser, Robert, 'Running With The Devil: Power, Gender, and Madness in Heavy Metal Music', Middletown: Wesleyan University Press. 1993

Wethington, William. "Britt Lightning soloing on Stranglehold I was singing" December 31,2022. 0:31. https://youtu.be/9coVESbkzhc

From Saris to Soul Food: A Rhetorical Comparative Essay

Mohamed Irhabi

Remember your ancestors? Probably not, but this is what they did so you can exist today: your ancestors fought fierce Indochinese tigers, wrestled grizzly bears, and survived tooth infections, all in the relentless pursuit of preserving their beliefs, traditions, and culture. Perhaps, you may have inherited a necklace, a piece of art, or a valuable gift that is evidence of their hardships; a tangible item that you can feel and experience. Thankfully, we are in a world removed from the wild nature and hard terrain our ancestors had to go through barefoot—we are presented with a new challenge: preserving what they inherited us with. This brings us to the narrative illustrated in "Cutting Our Grandmother's Saris" by Chandrasekaran and "Soul Food" by Hall. Both works dive into the preservation of cultural heritage and the evolution of traditions. "Cutting Our Grandmother's Saris" by Chandrasekaran and "Soul Food" by Hall both illustrate that, while cultural heritage and tradition serve as important points in our lives, it is also important to adapt and reinterpret them, to make sure that they are relevant in this modern world.

Moving on from the struggles of our ancestors, we can focus on the personal narratives of Chandrasekaran and Hall. Both Chandrasekaran and Hall use personal narratives to create an ethos of authenticity and credibility, drawing the reader to their cultural heritage. Chandrasekaran's narrative is focused on personal experience. Each descriptive imagery is a demonstration of her connection with her cultural roots; a connection that is portrayed through the lens of her grandmother's saris. When she states, "The stains and scents were evidence of the life she had lived, so different from my own," we are not just reading about a piece of fabric, rather we are told about the struggles and love of the stain and scent (Chandrasekaran 96). The detailed imagery and personal connection establish her credibility by discussing the emotional significance carried by the cultural artifacts. In comparison, Hall connects with readers through her deep experiences with soul food. She states, "I got that soul food in my bones. I was born into it in the South, with roots that go back generations" (Hall 417). These assertive statements show her authority in the lived experience, developing her ethos. Therefore, the authors use personal narratives to draw the reader in while creating an ethos of authenticity.

Building upon the foundation of credibility, the authors embed elements of pathos to draw the reader's attention to the emotional connections. Chandrasekaran and Hall appeal to pathos effectively to explain the emotional connections associated with cultural artifacts, but while Chandrasekaran focuses on the preservation of physical items, Hall stresses the revival of traditional food. Chandrasekaran's interpretation of her resistance to cutting the saris is loaded with emotion, "that this fabric—so soft, so luxurious—had caressed my grandmother's skin... and that my cut, once made, would forever alter that sari's potential" (Chandrasekaran 97). In contrast, Hall's expressive language fills soul food with cultural depth, as indicated when she says, "Soul food is the true food of African Americans" (Hall 418). She does not merely describe a cuisine but embeds cultural depth. Thus, using emotional connections associated with cultural artifacts, the authors appealed to pathos effectively; they evoked strong feelings and used vivid imagery to engage the reader with the author's feelings, making the authors' arguments more powerful.

The authors have established a strong sense of credibility and emotional connection with the reader. Now, they will rationalize their emotional claims by bridging feeling and reason. Both Chandrasekaran and Hall appeal to logos by presenting detailed historical and contextual information to explain the evolution of their culture, yet they focus on different things—Chandrasekaran on the personal/family, and Hall on the African American community. For example, Chandrasekaran's detailed description of her grandmother's life and the intrinsic value associated with the saris shows her argument about their symbolic significance: "Hers was a life of cooking curries, wearing turmeric, walking barefoot on dusty floors..." (Chandrasekaran 97). She provides specific examples from her grandmother's life, appealing to logos by connecting the emotional and symbolic meaning of the saris to real, tangible experiences.

In navigating this world, both narratives highlight the resistance or uncertainty faced by those who wish to reshape and modernize a cultural tradition. Both authors highlight the tension between preservation and adaptation; the emotional pull of preserving and the logical need to adapt. When Chandrasekaran told her aunt of her intentions of making a quilt out of her grandmother's sari, her aunt "was incredulous. These saris were valuable, meant to be worn, not cut" (Chandrasekaran 96). There is clear tension and resistance between the author and her aunt when her aunt tells her to preserve this symbolic inheritance. Hall engages with the audience with a rhetorical question, asking "'What's the difference between Southern food and soul food?'" (Hall 418). She provides a decisive and assertive answer: "Easy answer: black cooks." (Hall 418). This interaction between the author and reader prompts an understanding of the cultural origin that shapes this cuisine. Thus, the authors highlight the tension between preservation and adaptation via relatable experiences.

Having been through the authors' ethos, pathos, logos, and the tensions of preservation and adaptation, it is essential to honor our cultural traditions and heritage, and it is also important to adapt and reshape them to ensure they remain relevant. Chandrasekaran and Hall, through their use of ethos, pathos, and logos, have painted a great picture of the emotional, historical, and logical aspects of cultural evolution. Both "Cutting Our Grandmother's Saris" by Chandrasekaran and "Soul Food" by Hall illustrate that, while cultural heritage and tradition serve as important points in our lives, it is also important to adapt and reinterpret them—to ensure that these cultures continue its relevancy in the modern era.

Works Cited

Carla, Hall. "Soul Food." *The Norton Sampler, Ninth Edition.* W. W. Norton, 2018, p. 417.

Chandrasekaran, Priya. "Cutting Our Grandmothers' Saris." *The Norton Sampler, Ninth Edition.* W. W. Norton, 2019, p. 96.

Intellectual Filth: Nazification and Resistance at the University of Munich

Brandon Stumpf
Rowe Award for Scholarly Essay

In 1942, at Ludwig Maximilian University in Munich, Germany, student Sophie Scholl accidentally spilled anti-Nazi leaflets over the university building's balustrade, attracting the attention of university caretaker Jakob Schmid. Realizing that she and her brother Hans Scholl were distributing the leaflets, Schmid dutifully turned the siblings over to the Nazi secret police for interrogation. In these leaflets, the Scholls, three other LMU students, and a professor, identifying themselves as the White Rose organization, defied Nazi threats and published their grievances in a series of pamphlets that goaded ideologically enslaved Germans to "make an assault upon evil where it is strongest." They condemned the Hitler regime as "an irresponsible clique of rulers driven by their darkest urges" at a time when the government strictly censored dissenting opinions about the Nazis. The White Rose circle published and distributed six pamphlets between 1942 and 1943 before their arrest, and though their organization consisted of only six individuals, their story reaches far beyond their plight at the University of Munich.[1]

Were German universities bastions of Nazism? According to some scholarly works, German universities during the Nazi peacetimes (1933-39), were impotent and insignificant institutions and had been since the 1920s. According to this interpretation, the Nazi seizure of power in 1933 mainly just magnified their pre-existing dysfunction. In 2022, an anthology compiled topics like the interference and repositioning of German scholars during the transition from the Weimar Republic to the Nazi years in detail. One contribution put professors' "denazification surveys" on trial, saying professors with "good reasons to be worried" did not see the "brutal politics and practices and attack on academic freedom" as unacceptable. Another book argues that professors were most often Nationalists already or had to be to "get ahead" in universities as early as 1898. This position's evidence can be found in the Lex Anson case in which a professor was stripped of his *venia legendi* (authorization to teach) for simply being a social democrat. Other works claim that German academia created an atmosphere where nationalistic movements could claim to be a spiritual revival. It seems as if most literature revolves around crediting or discrediting the convention that there were primarily three camps of professors: those who were evil opportunity seekers who embraced Nazism; those who passively continued to justify themselves to a patron for paychecks;

and a few who outright protested Hitler. The problem with existing scholarship on German universities during the Nazi-period is that it neglects to construct a digestible narrative of the University of Munich's Nazification, its role in the White Rose's tragic end, and the White Rose's plight as a unique reflection of the University of Munich. The case study of the University of Munich provides a more complex narrative about the Nazification of German universities because, while it embraced the Nazi project, it also played host to resistance groups like the White Rose organization on campus.[2]

Although the university ultimately failed to protect its students and faculty, LMU achieved global recognition as a hospitably progressive and prestigious research institution. Its reputation preceded itself on an international basis, housing eight Nobel Prize laureates in chemistry and physics from 1901 to 1939. It was originally founded in 1472 by Duke Ludwig IX (the Wealthy) as the second university in the Altbayern region of Bavaria, and the eleventh university in the territories of the Holy Roman Empire. Despite its success in academia over the centuries, the nationalistic tendencies in the University of Munich became evident when the university senate refused to hold a ceremony for the adoption of the Weimar constitution. Eventually, the political atmosphere at the University of Munich displayed unwavering allegiance to the cause of National Socialism, demonstrated when caretaker Schmid turned the Scholls in to the Gestapo, prompting their interrogation on February 13, 1943, for simply writing and distributing dissenting opinions against the German government. The Ludwig Maximilian University of Munich betrayed principles the White Rose refused to forfeit when it purged its faculty and students' personal liberties, leaving a navigable process for its Nazification. Ideological surveying became an important role adopted by administrators, insidiously resembling Nazi bureaucrats as they forbade researchers to contradict Nazi ideals. LMU participated in quasi-religious book burnings that demonstrated the consequences for ideas that did not align with National Socialism. If the book burnings were their apotheosis, it brought the White Rose into their Holocaust of ideas.[3]

Though his research in Nazi Germany preceded the Scholls' capture at LMU, Edward Yarnall Hartshorne, Jr., brought the conversation surrounding cultural revolutions in Nazi-era higher education to the English-speaking world by compiling and translating statistical data, literature, science, and legislation. A sociology tutor from Harvard, Hartshorne described the "post 1918" Prussian student body in German universities as nationalistic when they advocated to unify all German speaking peoples in Europe within a single boundary. His report sometimes directly documented information

188

compiled on LMU. Even when it did not, the university's complex history as the sixth oldest research university in Germany and its location in the town where the Nazi party was founded made it a cultural centerpiece during the Nazi period. When the White Rose pamphlets and the story of the organization's resistance is reflected as a part of the university's history, it raises questions about the degree to which the university atmosphere inspired or oppressed the actions of the White Rose resistance. Juxtaposing Nazi-era German laws and the White Rose resistance with Hartshorne's data on German universities during the Nazi period permits the University of Munich to serve as a map of Nazification in all German institutions of higher education because it captures such political diversity in spirit and intellect.[4]

Hitler came into office as chancellor of Germany on January 30, 1933, though the reverberations of his inauguration were most intensely felt a month later, on February 28, with the Reichstag Fire Decree, and March 25, through the Enabling Act. The Fire Decree disposed of Germans' "personal liberty," abrogating the values the Weimar Constitution held inviolable, like rights to freely print, speak, and assemble, and the freedom to express or challenge ideas. The constitution enshrined personal liberties, free speech, and the equal treatment of women. Hitler utilized the precedent of Germany's Achilles heel clause, Article 48, of the Weimar Constitution to pass the Enabling Act, which unraveled the democratic procedures and checks and balances established in Articles 68-77 of the Weimar Constitution.[5] Germany's instability during the Weimar era aside, its constitution offered German universities the latitude to flourish intellectually. Though plagued with high rates of unemployment, Germany enjoyed a period called the "Golden Ages" between 1924 and 1929, that has been compared to the United States' "Roaring Twenties," when economic progress was made and foreign relations somewhat smoothed over.[6]

The Enabling Act circumvented the "people's" republic and solidified Hitler's power to pass laws resistant to legislative or con-stitutional counterweight. Hitler's clandestine plot to minimize legislative power in the Reichstag body governed by the Weimar Constitution allowed his regime to assume hegemony over all public assemblies, publications, and parades in a quest to silence dissent-ing opinion. This feature laid the foundation for Hitler's passing of legislation that specifically targeted Jewish or otherwise allegedly undesirable individuals from education, especially higher educa-tion, where the regime aimed to imbue young adults and professors with Nazism.[7]

Using the Enabling Act, on April 25, 1933, the Hitler regime published the Law Against Overcrowding in the government gazette *Reichsgesetzblatt*. The measure gave the Hitler regime the ability to choose university students and faculty based on their commitment to National Socialism. Pursuant with the aim of *Gleichschaltung* in universities, which sought to unify universities with the Nazi state, the laws targeted mostly Jewish students, as Nazis considered Jews the most foreign of foreigners, whether inside or outside of the educational sphere. A table created by Dr. Charlotte Luetkens in 1939 showed that total German enrollments in university winter sessions dropped precipitously from 122,847 in 1932-33 to 71,850 in 1936-37, a decrease of more than 40 percent. This was just the beginning of a series of racial and legal cultural revolutions overrunning the humanities and sciences in Germany. Enabling these cultural revolutions were legal frameworks that attempted to unify the German universities, such as the University of Munich, and the Third Reich into one large Nazi organization.[8]

The "Action Against the Un-German Spirit" proclamation made by the National Socialist German Student Union in 1933 has been widely documented as responsible for the quasi-religious book burnings orchestrated across German universities. The largest and most notorious book burning at Opera Square, Berlin, where Minister of Enlightenment and Propaganda Joseph Goebbels spoke personally, has eclipsed many of the other book burnings, like the one held in Königsplatz Square in Munich. Though LMU's explanation on their website strictly claims that no official university faculty participated in the book burning, certainly none successfully stepped in to prevent students from ransacking libraries and burning copious amounts of literature.[9]

One of the National Socialist German Student Union's first implementations of this incendiary strategy was to burn the library of Magnus Hirschfeld, director of the Institute of Sex Research. Archives of around 20,000 books burned publicly in the streets on May 6, 1933. Its collections and topics ranged from homosexuality to transgender studies. Four days later, the student union se 25,000 volumes of un-German books ablaze in Opera Square, Berlin, across from Humboldt University. More than 5000 students gathered for this book burning. A cursory list of authors burned included Heinrich Mann, Arnold and Stefan Zweig, Erich Maria Remarque, Karl Marx, Lion Feuchtwanger, Kurt Tucholsky, Erich Kästner, Carl von Ossietzky, Thomas Mann, Albert Einstein, and Sigmund Freud. The goal behind this intellectual cleansing was to show what happened to ideas that did not align with National Socialist values, embraced by Hitler's writings and speeches. It set the precedent for universities like LMU to dismiss un-German "intellectual filth into the flames" and enabled scholars to begin fulfilling Hitler's antisemitic policies by assuming the "responsibility of removing this garbage and clearing the path for truly German works."[10]

Comparatively, the University of Munich's predominately politically driven transition into the Nazi period looked different than at other universities, at least initially. Scholars have pointed out that, in such cases as the University of Gottingen, Humboldt, and Berlin, the hiring process in universities shifted from a democratic electoral system to political appointments in a top-down fashion that prioritized those politically affiliated with the Nazi party. Eugene Mattiat, a theologian in Germany who involved himself heavily in politics, gained a post in the Ministry of Education and became chief advisor for academic appointments in the humanities all over Germany. To complete the masquerade that he was qualified for such a position, Nazi politicians appointed him professor and chair of *Volkskunde*, or German "folklore," at the University of Gottingen without consulting the university at all. Mattiat used his post unscientifically and unmethodically to elicit awareness and appreciation of "Germanness" through language, race, and history. On a separate occasion, the Nazi government imposed a new rector on the University of Berlin who had "few acquaintances among his teachers in his own university, since in his thirty-seven years of life he had never published anything" noteworthy. The rector, however, performed his assigned duty of pushing Nazi programs and frequently spoke about bolstering Nazi ideals, weeding out Jewish blood, and calling for professors and students to rally behind the new university spirit.[11]

The federal laws permitting these Nazis to play educator or administrator were strategically placed and exceedingly politicized. They created an environment where dilettantes with Nazi gusto could worm their way into positions of power in higher education, such as through the Law Against Overcrowding, but Hitler was equally concerned with the youth and young adults' ideological education, or lack thereof, in Germany. To sow future antisemites and Hitler ideologues, on December 28, 1933, the Minister of the Interior, sought to fulfill the "law combatting the overcrowding of the secondary and higher schools" passed the previous April. He declared a scant 15,000 as the maximal number of admissions for all of higher education in Germany for the 1934-1935 school year. Hartshorne calculated the number of admissions the year prior to the admission cap and determined the 1933-1934 school year yielded about 20,000 admissions. Bavaria, the home province of the University of Munich accounted for 1,670 of them.[12] Capping the maximal amount of admissions at 15,000 meant an inaugural 25 percent decrease in German student admissions during 1934-1935 compared to the previous school year.[13]

This empirical evidence contextualizes the politicization of the admission process enacted in the early days of Hitler's Germany. The admission cap afforded the regime latitude to install "politically reliable" functionaries throughout German higher education. The new laws changed the criteria for considering candidates' admission into university. The director first selected candidates based on their physical, moral-political, racial, and intellectual standings. Final admission depended upon the "Director of the Division for Higher Education for the Provincial Ministry, who makes the final decision, but only after he discusses the 'political reliability' of the candidate with the local leader" of the Nazi Party. A last check prior to their admission was to require student candidates to present evidence of their service to the Nazi state. The tell-tale signs of a passionate Nazi supposedly made them easily distinguishable, and the admissions filters the Nazis put into place worked exceedingly well. Nevertheless, as the freedom seekers in the White Rose proved, the state could not suppress their liberty, despite Hitler's ambitious efforts.[14]

Hans and Sophie Scholl and the rest of the White Rose circle were unsuccessfully intellectually filtered, despite the rigorous policies in place at the University of Munich. Underscoring her uncompromising nature, Sophie wrote one word, "freedom," on a copy of her court indictment, which marked her final act of defiance while she awaited her fate, trapped in a cell. As headstrong as she was, she was equally witty and desirous of a liberal education. Her capacity for abstract thought and her broad-minded character led her to follow her brother's footsteps, by enrolling at LMU in 1942. Like fellow member Christoph Probst, Hans Scholl completed his seven months of compulsory labor service and basic military training in order to begin studying at the University of Munich in April 1939. Hans connected with Professor Kurt Huber, who played a foundational role in the White Rose mission. The Ministry of the Interior and Education also failed to detect him, since he taught at LMU from 1921 until his arrest. He wrote a letter to his wife, Clara, the day of his capture. It outlined his alleged "political unreliability" and captured the essence of the scholar. "If I should suffer death in the fight for freedom" he wrote, "rejoice and be glad at one who has found his way home in the ultimate freedom of the spirit. Giving up my life will have made me completely free." Another White Rose member, Alexander Schmorell, began studying at LMU in 1940, followed by Willi Graf who began in April of 1942. Both had served alongside Hans Scholl at the Russian front in the autumn of 1942. These members possessed the bravery and wisdom required of individuals who managed to persevere in their independent thinking despite a life of political indoctrination by Nazis.[15]

Along with caretaker Schmid, the university rector was also involved in the decision to hand Hans and Sophie Scholl over to the Gestapo. LMU gained its own Nazi cult of personality on campus in rector Walter Wüst. Serving as rector of the university from 1941 to 1945, he was a much more vigorous academic than those like Eugene Mattiat. His personal papers at the LMU archive show that he began studying German, English, Indian philology, and comparative religions at the University of Munich in 1920. In 1923, he completed his doctoral thesis and in 1926 underwent "habilitation," the standard hiring procedure in German universities for professor candidates. The dean of the philosophy department at the University of Munich, Lucian Sherman, congratulated him on his philological excellence, and by 1935 Wüst held a full professorship at the University of Munich. He became an avid lecturer, giving a keynote at the East Asia Mission annual meeting, and a board member, editor, and frequent publisher for the *Journal of Mission Studies and Religious Studies*, or *Zeitschrift für Missionskunde und Religionswissenschaft*.[16]

In 1935, Wüst was aspiring to join a program that SS leader Heinrich Himmler and conspiracy theorist-academic Herman Wirth co-founded on July 1, 1935, called *Ahnenerbe*. Wirth fabricated a book at the end of 1933 called the *Ura-Linda-Chronik*, which he claimed encompassed texts and symbols that dated to the third century BCE. Wirth promoted awareness of unfounded conspiracy theories surrounding ancient Nordic civilizations, while fabricating a history that replaced Christianity's Jewish origins with primeval Nordic myths. Himmler readily embraced a crackpot theorist camouflaged as an academic whose ideas furthered Nazi antisemitism. Wüst capitalized on the opportunity to become acquainted with Himmler. At Wirth's urging, Wüst reached out to Himmler with a letter demonstrating his humble, submissive, and obsequious nature. Himmler approved of him, and Wüst joined the *Ahnenerbe*, coincidentally the same year that he received the full professorship at the University of Munich overseeing the Study of Aryan Culture and Language.[17]

Walter Wüst's story as a seemingly "ordinary," hardworking, yet opportunistic academic sheds light on the atmosphere at the University of Munich and implies that at a certain point during LMU's cultural and legal adaptation to Nazism, it was better for professors' careers at Munich to support conspiracy theories, including Wirth's stone age Nordic civilizations and fictitious religions. Wüst began teaching Indian philology at LMU in 1926, prior to the Nazi consolidation of power, and Hartshorne's report showed that, at the time, the university operated in compliance with the

Richter-Peter Statutes of 1924 to 1929. In 1926, LMU vested tangible power in the faculty, giving them a certain degree of autonomy. The democratic electoral system was commonly practiced in university operations, but by 1935-1936 Hartshorne already described it in his report as "the old system." The university was divided into its primary faculties, like law, medicine, philosophy, and theology, and organized "each under a dean of its own election." The faculties were bestowed the power of the "authorization of the young Ph.D. as an instructor . . . [and] the proposal for the promotion of instructors to higher ranks, and. . . the proposal for calling of men from other universities to positions on their own faculty." Their autonomy was exemplified in their authority to conduct habilitation and promotion and to propose new appointments to their own faculty. Though this style of university government was short-lived in the early twentieth century, it exhibited the democratic undertones in German society through the Weimar period.[18]

Hartshorne not only documented this "old system," or what could be interpreted as the Weimar era's status quo of university operations, but also provided thorough coverage of the legislation that radically modified university systems under the National Socialists. He called these the "Nazi Revisions." In either 1935 or 1936, Hartshorne included an English translation of the new official governing rules of higher education, those contemporaneous to his work in Nazi Germany. These rules were promulgated on April 3, 1935, and though not stated directly in the report, were likely posted from an organization like the SS or Ministry of Education. They were called the "Guiding Principles for the Simplification of University Administration" and captured the character of the officials in charge of Nazi-era German universities. The rules paralleled how the country was transitioning from its democratic roots planted in the Weimar era, to the authoritarian frameworks constructed by the Nazis. According to clause four, "The Rektor is the Führer of the University, directly subordinate to the Minister of Education and to him alone." In clause five, "The Leader (Leiter of the *Dozentenschaft*) is named by the Minister of Education after consultation with the Rector and with the Local Leader (*Gauführer*) of the National Socialist University Teachers Union (NS *Dozentenbund*), and is directly responsible to the Rector." The edict in which habilitation, the process under the old system in which faculty decided to confer or reject candidates with their *venia legendi* (right to teach), was altered as well, so that "every decision of the faculty conferring the right to teach requires the approval of the Minister." The latter change was a severe modification from the Richter-Peters statutes and a brash undermining of faculty autonomy. Power was carefully nestled at the top of the university, vested in an autocratic rector who answered only to the Minister of Education, who himself was directly responsible to the Nazi federal government. The rector's authority substantially outweighed that of any faculty in terms of habilitation, promotion, and appointment. This 1935 model replaced the trust universities placed in peer review and abrogated the liberties previously enjoyed through academic merit, supplanting them with a system pursuant to the aim of *Gleichschaltung*. Such reorganizations of the political, scientific, and financial technologies in the university predisposed the University of Munich to exert the brutal censorship policies that led to the seizure and arrest of the members of the White Rose organization and the oppression of any other forms of denunciation of the Nazis' treatment of Jews or their dissemination of lies disguised as truth.[19]

An insightful glimpse at a 1919 letter Hitler wrote concerning Germany's antisemitism illuminates the situation in 1936 at LMU. Hitler displayed concerns over Germany's tenets of antisemitism, describing them as emotionally driven. He instead proposed a new and improved variety of "antisemitism grounded in reason." Hitler believed this upgraded brand of antisemitism should be founded scientifically and based on race, to the extent that his eighth-grade-equivalent education allowed. Hitler's primary complaint was that the current antisemitism meandered between religion and culture instead of race. In 1933, the regime legitimized and financed an interdisciplinary field called *Judenforschung*. One of the Nazi *Judenforschung's* tenets was that that Jewish life and history had been inherently biased because it was mostly documented by Jews. Although it never became a full-fledged academic discipline, primarily because of Germany's defeat in World War II, it was sustained through networking scholars, research institutions, and academic journals. The Nazi regime utilized government connections to bridge the gap between state and academia, evident by the establishment of the Research Department of the Institute for the History of the New Germany, affiliated with the University of Munich. It also published a journal called *Research for the Jewish Question* that hosted new scholarship written by antisemitic scholars for the sake of *Judenforschung*. By recognizing *Judenforschung*, it seemed like the regime had launched into undertaking the ideas Hitler proposed in his letter, promoting an antisemitism grounded in and propped up by academia. *Judenforschung* gained more traction in 1936 and was headed by LMU history professor Wilhem Grau. Among its efforts to garner support, the department facilitated conferences, one notably in 1936 at the University of Munich, where Professor Karl Alaxander Von Müller of the University of Munich, a nationalistic antisemite, was the keynote speaker.[20]

A contemporary who studied under Müller, Walter Frank of the University of Munich, also spoke at the Research Department of the Institute for the History of the New Germany conference at the university, highlighting one of the central goals for the LMU and for the rest of German higher education. In his speech, he highlighted some of the missions of their organization when he said, "only one side of the Jewish problem has been addressed, the Jewish side; almost all books on the Jewish question have been written by Jews." In this, he meant to dismiss Jewish history as problematic, because it had been mostly written by Jews and therefore contained a Jewish bias hostile towards Germans. The Jewish Question existed because Jewish history had been written by Jews, which Nazi academics saw as an inherent disservice to the humanities. A central goal of Müller, Frank, and Grau in their research department was to challenge the historiography of Jewish history because of its supposed pro-Jewish leanings. Later in the same speech, Walter Frank admitted that "dissertations on the Jewish question have been submitted almost entirely by Jews; the historical Journals have selected only Jews as editors for matters Jewish." The Research Department pushed to reinvent Jewish history through a German lens by "curing" the historiographical errors in Jewish history, ultimately by erasing Jewish historians, overcoming culturally based antisemitism, and confirming race as the most important factor in the quality of scholarship. The University of Munich in 1936 cannot be discussed without mentioning that it hosted these National Socialists ideas and conferences. Though scholars had already published overtly antisemitic works while working at LMU prior to this new department, the conference afforded a gross display of academic commitment to Nazism, and subsequently, *Judenforschung*.[21]

Despite the vicious antisemitic organizations and research departments taking hold at LMU, it was initially more resilient than other Nazi-era German universities to the immediate dismissal of faculty upon the Nazis' seizure of power. Hartshorne's data shows that, upon the Nazi seizure of power in 1933, the University of Munich sustained thirty-two dismissals out of the 387 faculty members, excluding assistants, for a staggering 8.2 percent loss of its total faculty. Compared to some schools, like the University of Berlin, which lost 242 out of 746. 32.4 percent, LMU fared well. The data does not provide details about which departments lost the most faculty at LMU, but Hartshorne's numbers do show that medicine and social science departments lost the most scholars nationwide. Across Germany, medicine accounted for 412 of the total 1,615 faculty dismissals (26 percent), and social sciences 173 (11 percent). History followed with sixty scholars dismissed. Hartshorne was also able to determine that 896 dismissals were "known cases," meaning in which the grounds for dismissal are known. Of those 230 scholars (26 percent) were "definitely Non-Aryan." By the end of the war in 1945, there is no concrete statistic on how many faculty had been fired because of National Socialism. The Nazi regime exiled more than 1,600 academics, yet others left on their own accord, in protest in 1933. The University of Berlin's rector retired because of the rise of the National Socialist movement. The evidence points out the complexities of the Nazi standard for determining "political unreliability." Dismissing scholars and deciding which universities to target heaviest proved more of an art than a science. If Berlin was the epicenter of the Nazi political movement, then Munich acted as a dystopian satellite for scholars in Germany.[22]

If the Nazis purged disloyal faculty, they also rooted out students with questionable politics, or allegedly undesirable racial qualities. Hartshorne's data tracks the reduction in enrollments at the University of Munich from winter session 1930 to summer session 1936. As expected from the trends revealed thus far, each year yielded lower enrollments. Hartshorne used the data to illustrate the Nazi guided dispersal of students from large universities to smaller rural colleges. Besides the advantage of hindsight, the immense amount of studying of Nazi Germany has allowed for careful contextualization. LMU's website offers a figure of 3000 to 4000 students enrolled between 1941 to 1945. This comfortably completes the trend Hartshorne identified, but left unfinished. He listed 8,229 enrollments at LMU during the winter session 1934 to 1935, then a steep drop to 5,000 in summer session 1935, and then a slight increase to 5,200 in summer session 1936. Further racial and intellectual filtering of the universities, alongside the beginning of the war in September of 1939 further explain why the enrollments "fell drastically," according to LMU's data.[23]

The state of the German universities was subject to the temperamental Nazi government now inextricably intertwined with them. LMU's website shows their enrollments fell to devastatingly low figures during the 1940s. The lack of students was partially due to the worsening conditions on the Eastern Front. The German military's offensive failures against the Soviets demanded an increasing amount of warm bodies to put on the battlefield. Though the initial attack on Leningrad and Moscow seemed optimistic for the Germans, as time passed from 1941 to the mid-1940s, so did the ever-increasing death toll. This was likely discouraging to the general populace of student-aged men. German optimism began fading quickly as the death count rose and as they failed to establish reliable transportation routes for sending materials to the front lines.

Hitler himself gave his "last great public speech" while the battle for Stalingrad raged on November 8, 1942. In the speech, he acknowledged the advantages of keeping "the war as far away as possible" from the German homeland. If the people were isolated, far away from the tens of thousands dying on the war fronts, they could remain as oblivious as possible, salve their consciences through ignorance, and sleep soundly while continuing their support for Hitler. Hitler claimed intrinsic advantages over his enemies because the German people ideologically supported him and the German army as a "National Socialist Party [and] as a dedicated community," regardless of the German military's deteriorating material conditions.[24]

Three students at the University of Munich who belonged to the White Rose organization had served on the Eastern Front and had seen the atrocities of the war. Their firsthand accounts likely influenced their decisions to take part in speaking out against the Nazi regime. Their writings suggest as much. The second White Rose pamphlet, unlike their colleagues' *Research for the Jewish Question* journal, refused to participate in any discussion of the Jewish Question, likely because "a plea of defense" dignified the antisemitism as a concept. Instead, the author of the second pamphlet pointed to the German's war in Poland and underscores the point that "three hundred thousand Jews have been murdered in that country in the most bestial manner." The pamphlets worked to humanize the Jews and to show how absurd Germany's deeply seated antisemitic values were, using the Nazi regime's language against them, and criticizing its actions as the work of "subhumanity." The second pamphlet used powerful language, calling upon Germans to realize how complicit they were in their apathy. The White Rose understood that it was the moral duty of the German people to launch into resistance against the Nazis for their crimes. Any ideological support for the regime was in fact a grave crime that fostered a collective guilt that implicated every passive German. "GUILTY GUILTY GUILTY!" they wrote, before reassuring Germans that "it is not too late to rid the world of the most heinous monstrosity of a government." They could redeem themselves by undertaking "the most sacred duty...to destroy these [Nazi] beasts!"[25]

None of the students in the White Rose were over the age twenty-five when their organization was discovered and their cover blown. The oldest of the students, Alexander Schmorell, was born around the end of Germany's defeat in World War I in 1918. Their youngest years and adolescence were met with severe political instability and viciously antisemitic, xenophobic Nazi rhetoric. Each member, except the professor, participated in the Nazis' compulsory training at young ages. They were impressionable teenagers when Germany received Hitler as chancellor in 1933. Their peers won large majorities in the National Socialists' student bodies, and they never had a vote or a say in who governed them. It is not only because of their persevering through their upbringing that makes the White Rose at the University of Munich so striking, but how it exposes the true limitations of the Nazi's ability to subdue a society through laws and fear-mongering.

Judenforchung and the *Ahnenerbe* were short lived because of the Allies' victory in World War II. The University of Munich played host to these anti-intellectual organizations but also secreted the White Rose organization. Individuals like Walter Wüst and Müller, who welcomed Nazi censorship and legitimized the hatred that contributed to the Holocaust, passed Hans and Sophie Scholl, and the rest of the White Rose circle in the halls of LMU. Their differences are overwhelming. Still, no amount of Nazi filtering at the University of Munich could snuff out the bravery and resilience of those in the White Rose. After distributing what became the last installment of White Rose pamphlets in the main university building at the Ludwig Maximilian University of Munich, they were captured and charged with high treason for "supporting the enemy" on February 13, 1943. The Scholl siblings and their student and teacher allies never lived to see the Germans awaken. Four days after they were captured, on February 22, they were executed at the guillotine for their clandestine plots to enlighten their neighbors. Alongside them at the guillotine was student Christoph Probst, a twenty-three-year-old father of three, who aided in writing and distributing the pamphlets. The Nazis executed three other members of the White Rose—two students and a professor—later that year. The history of the University of Munich cannot be assembled without careful explanation of their role in the Third Reich's educational sphere. Their story is one that reaches far beyond the context of Nazi Germany, though, and beckons the passion of those who freely think, reawakening their core philosophies when, inevitably, adversaries try to censor them. The White Rose circle reminds the world that free thinkers will always manage a way, despite the state's greatest effort to bankrupt its population of personal liberty. Ultimately, the case of the University of Munich cannot be forgotten wherever and whenever the lines between government, educational institutions, and personal liberty blur.[26]

Endnotes

[1] Alexandra Lloyd, comp., *Defying Hitler: The White Rose Pamphlets* (Oxford: Bodleian Library, 2022), 4, 91.

[2] Lloyd, *Defying Hitler*, greatly contributed to bringing the conversation of Nazi-era German universities, and the plight of the White Rose Circle at the University of Munich to the English-speaking world by compiling and translating the White Rose pamphlets into English and mapping their resistance story. See Alan E. Steinweis, "Nazi Historical Scholarship on the Jewish Question," in *Nazi Germany and the Humanities: How German Academics Embraced Nazism*, ed. Wolfgand Bialas and Anson Rabinbach (London: Oneworld Publications, 2007), 399-412, for startling accounts of antisemitic departments on campuses during the Nazi period. Charles E. McClelland, "The German University and Its Influence," *The Oxford Handbook of the History of Education* (Oxford: Oxford University Press, 2019), 274–88, offers a brief but complete history of German higher education. Fritz K. Ringer, *The Decline of the German Mandarins: The German Academic Community, 1890-1933* (Hanover: University Press of New England, 1990), offers history and elemental insight into the culture of German universities in relation to the German state at the cusp of the Hitler era with great sociological vigor. Edward Yarnall Hartshorne, *The German Universities and National Socialism* (Cambridge: Harvard University Press, 1937), was published in the trenches of the war on German universities and provides valuable primary source material in English. M. Levinson and Robert P. Ericksen, *The Betrayal of the Humanities: The University during the Third Reich* (Bloomington: Indiana University Press, 2022), is a recent collaborative work and unprecedented feat of scholarship surrounding the Nazification and the deeply complex social makeup of German academia around the Nazi years. Alice Gallin, *Midwives to Nazism: University Professors in Weimar Germany, 1925-1933* (Macon, GA: Mercer University Press, 1986) argues that professors were disparaging of their less nationalistic colleagues, heralds of Nazism, and therefore "bedfellows" with the radical National Socialist Student Organization whom they despised for their vulgarity and clownish behavior.

[3] Ludwig Maximilian University of Munich, "Nobel Prizes," https://www.lmu.de/en/about-lmu/lmu-at-a-glance/

awards/nobel-prize/index.html (accessed October 8, 2023); LMU, "1918-1945: The Weimar Republic and the Nazi Period," https://www.lmu.de/en/about-lmu/lmu-at-a-glance/history/contexts/1918-1945-the-weimar-republic-and-the-nazi-period/index.html (accessed September 25, 2023); Hartshorne, *German Universities and National Socialism*, 44.

[4] LMU Munich, "1918-1945: The Weimar Republic and the Nazi Period."

[5] Article 48 of the Weimar Constitution vested emergency dictatorial powers in the president, which President Paul Von Hindenburg exercised excessively, undermining checks and balances established in the constitution.

[6] Weimar Constitution, art. 48, sec. 3; Weimar Constitution art. 68-77, sec. 5; United States Holocaust Memorial Museum, "The Enabling Act," https://encyclopedia.ushmm.org/content/en/article/the-enabling-act (accessed July 19, 2023); United States Holocaust Memorial Museum, "Reichstag Fire Decree." https://encyclopedia.ushmm.org/content/en/article/reichstag-fire-decree?series=40 (accessed July 19, 2023); The Wienar Holocaust Library, "The Weimar Republic," *The Golden Years—The Holocaust Explained: Designed for schools*, https://www.theholocaustexplained.org/the-nazi-rise-to-power/the-weimar-republic/golden-years/ (accessed July 20, 2023.)

[7] United States Holocaust Memorial Museum, "Reichstag Fire Decree."

[8] Hartshorne, *German Universities and National Socialism* 14, 15; The Law Against Overcrowding, Bundesarchive Berlin, R43II/936, United States Holocaust Memorial Museum, Washington DC; Charlotte Luetkens, "Enrolments at German Universities since 1933," *The Sociological Review* A31, no. 2 (1939), 94; United States Holocaust Memorial Museum, "The Enabling Act."

[9] United States Holocaust Memorial Museum, "Book Burning."

[10] Steven E. Aschheim, *At the Edges of Liberalism: Junctions of European, German, and Jewish History* (New York: Palgrave Macmillan, 2012), 117, 118; Ralf Georg Reuth, *Goebbels: The Life of Joseph Goebbels, the Mephistophelean Genius of Nazi Propaganda*, trans. Krishna Winston (London: Constable, 1995), 183.

[11] Robert P. Ericksen, *Complicity in the Holocaust: Churches and Universities in Nazi Germany* (New York: Cambridge University Press, 2012), 145, 146, 147; Hartshorne, *German*

Universities and National Socialism, 128, 129.

[12] Hartshorne's data shows that an estimated 10,000 students were rejected university entry in Germany during the 1933-1934 school year.

[13] Hartshorne, *Universities and National Socialism*, 79, 80.

[14] Hartshorne, *Universities and National Socialism*, 80.

[15] Lloyd, *Defying Hitler*, 63, 66, 69, 73,75-78, 82.

[16] ZMR, "Zeitschrift Für Missionswissenschaft Und Religionswissenschaft," Zeitschrift für Missionswissenschaft und Religionswissenschaft, https://www.unifr.ch/zmr/de/ (accessed November 11, 2023); Horst Junginger, "From Buddha to Adolf Hitler: Walther Wüst and the Aryan Tradition," in *The Study of Religion Under the Impact of Fascism*, ed. Horst Junginger, (Leiden: Brill, 2008), 105–177, 109.

[17] Junginger, "From Buddha to Adolf Hitler: Walther Wüst and the Aryan Tradition," 115-117.

[18] Hartshorne, *German Universities and National Socialism*, 47, 48, 49.

[19] Hartshorne, *German Universities and National Socialism*, 50, 51.

[20] Steinweis, "Nazi Historical Scholarship on the Jewish Question," 400, 401, 402.

[21] Steinweis, *Nazi Historical Scholarship on the Jewish Question*, 402, 403.

[22] Hartshorne, *German Universities and National Socialism*, 94, 99.

[23] Hartshorne, *German Universities and National Socialism*, 85; LMU, "The Changing Face of the LMU Student."

[24] R. Stackelberg and S. A. Winkle, *The Nazi Germany Sourcebook: An Anthology of Texts* (London: Routledge, 2002), 284, 295, 297.

[25] Lloyd, *Defying Hitler*, 98, 100.

[26] Lloyd, *Defying Hitler*, 4.

Bibliography

Primary Sources

"Aus Gottes eigenem Land." Das eherne Herz Munich: Zentralverlag der NSDAP, 1943.

Hartshorne, Edward Yarnall. *The German Universities and National Socialism*. Cambridge: Harvard University Press, 1937.

Kohlrausch, Eduard. May 5, 1933. Bundesarchiv Berlin. Berlin, Germany. https://perspectives.ushmm.org/item/telegram-regarding-the-action-against-the-un-german-spirit/collection/higher-education-in-nazi-germany. Accessed on September 20, 2023.

Law for the Reestablishment of the Professional Civil Service (April 7, 1933). In United States Chief Counsel for the Prosecution of Axis Criminality, *Nazi Conspiracy and Aggression*, Vol 3. Washington, DC: United States Government Printing Office, 1946, Document 1397-PS.

Lloyd, Alexandra, comp. *Defying Hitler: The White Rose Pamphlets*. Oxford: Bodleian Library, 2022.

Luetkens, Charlotte. "Enrolments at German Universities Since 1933." *The Sociological Review* A31, no. 2 (1939): 194-209.

Reichsgesetzblatt, Teil 1, April 7, 1933, S. 175. (Law For the Restoration of the Professional Civil Service).

Stackelberg, R., and S. A. Winkle. *The Nazi Germany Sourcebook: An Anthology of texts*. London: Routledge, 2002.

United States Holocaust Memorial Museum. "The Enabling Act." https://encyclopedia.ushmm.org/content/en/article/the-enabling-act. Accessed July 19, 2023.

——. "Nuremberg Race Laws." https://encyclopedia.ushmm.org/content/en/timeline-event/holocaust/1933-1938/nuremberg-race-laws. Accessed June 20, 2023.

——. "Reichstag Fire Decree." https://encyclopedia.ushmm.org/content/en/article/reichstag-fire-decree?series=40. Accessed July 19, 2023.

Weimar Constitution.

Secondary Sources

Aschheim, Steven E. *At the Edges of Liberalism: Junctions of European, German, and Jewish History*. New York: Palgrave Macmillan, 2012.

Biales Wolfgang, and Anson Rabinbach, eds. *Nazi Germany and the Humanities: How German Academics Embraced Nazism*. London: Oneworld Publications, 2007.

Gallin, Alice. Midwives to Nazism: *University Professors in Weimar Germany, 1925-1933*. Macon, GA: Mercer University Press, 1986.

Junginger, Horst. "From Buddha to Adolf Hitler: Walther Wüst and the Aryan Tradition." In *The Study of Religion Under the Impact of Fascism*, ed Horst Junginger, 105-177. Leiden: Brill, 2008.

Levinson, Bernard M., and Robert P. Ericksen, eds. *The Betrayal of the Humanities: The University During the Third Reich*. Bloomington: Indiana University Press, 2022.

Ludwig-Maximilians-Universität München. "1918-1945: The Weimar Republic and the Nazi Period," https://www.lmu.de/en/about-lmu/lmu-at-a-glance/history/contexts/1918-1945-the-weimar-republic-and-the-nazi-period/index.html. Accessed September 25, 2023.

——. "The Changing Face of the LMU Student." https://www.lmu.de/en/about-lmu/lmu-at-a-glance/history/contexts/the-changing-face-of-the-lmu-student/index.html. Accessed September 25.

——. "Nobel Prizes," https://www.lmu.de/en/about-lmu/lmu-at-a-glance/awards/nobel-prize/index.html. Accessed October 8, 2023.

McClelland, Charles E. "The German University and Its Influence." In *The Oxford Handbook of the History of Education*, ed. John L. Rury and Eileen H. Tamura, 274–88. Oxford: Oxford University Press, 2019.

Reuth, Ralf Georg. *Goebbels: The Life of Joseph Goebbels, the Mephistophelean Genius of Nazi Propaganda*. Translated by Krishna Winston. London: Constable, 1995.

Ringer, Fritz K. *The Decline of the German Mandarins: The German Academic Community, 1890-1933*. Hanover and London: University Press of New England, 1990.

Russel, James Earl. *German Higher Schools: The History, Organization and Methods of Secondary Education in Germany*. New York: Longmans, Green and Co., 1899.

Steinweis, Alan "Nazi Historical Scholarship on the Jewish Question." In *Nazi Germany and the Humanities: How German Academics Embraced Nazism*, ed. Wolfgand Bialas and Anson Rabinbach, 399-412. London: Oneworld Publications, 2007.

United States Holocaust Memorial Museum. "Book Burning." United States Holocaust Memorial Museum. https://encyclopedia.ushmm.org/content/en/article/book-burning. Accessed February 18, 2023.

The Wienar Holocaust Library. "The Weimar Republic." *The Golden Years—The Holocaust Explained: Designed for schools.* https://www.theholocaustexplained.org/the-nazi-rise-to-power/the-weimar-republic/golden-years/. Accessed July 20, 2023.

Biographies

Contributer Biographies

Esveiri Arteaga
Esveiri Arteaga is a DACA Dreamer and first gen college student of Beaumont, TX. She is currently pursuing a BS in Interdisciplinary Studies with a Concentration in EC-6 and a minor in Spanish. After graduation, she plans to be a bilingual teacher and eventually pursue a Masters in Elementary School counseling. During her free time, she spends time with her newly wedded husband and serves in children's and youth ministries in her church congregation. Her joy in life is serving her community and being a light in a world filled with darkness.

Patrick Blalack
Patrick Blalack is a Senior graduating with a Bachelor of Arts in May 2024. Beginning in Fall 2020 at East Tennessee State University, Patrick moved to Beaumont, Texas in May 2021 and transferred to Lamar University to continue his English degree. He takes a great interest in Literature, especially early British Literature and mythology

Daisy Calero Estrella
Daisy Calero Estrella is a nursing student from Port Arthur. She is involved in various student organizations, serving as HSA president and Junior Class Senator in SGA. She is excited to be featured in Pulse and hopes she will inspire non-English majors to rekindle a perhaps lost passion for poetry.

Robyn Gerry
Robyn Gerry is a senior history major and English minor at Lamar University. She is a classically trained violinist of eleven years, and also enjoys playing the piano. Robyn is also an archivist intern at the Tyrell Historical Library, currently working on the Jefferson Theatre Restoration Collection.

Gwendalyn Henning
Gwendalyn Henning is a full-time Mechanical Engineering student and full-time Civil PE assistant. She pulls her creative inspiration from artists like Hozier, Ethel Cain, and Mitski

Chassidy Hearn
Chassidy Hearn is a talented college student pursuing chemical engineering with a passion for poetry. Her piece "Senescence" showcases her ability to capture complex emotions in simple yet powerful language. Chassidy hopes to continue writing and sharing her work with others.

Benjamin Hernandez
Benjamin Hernandez is a sophomore here at Lamar University. He is majoring in history and minoring in anthropology. He aspires to be a history professor in the future. Benjamin was born and raised in Houston, Texas and has always had an interest in writing since

elementary school. He is inspired by the works of J.R.R. Tolkien, Johnny Cash, Willaim Shakespeare, and Frank Herbert. Benjamin even aspires to one day write and publish a novel.

Mohamed Irhabi

Mohamed Irhabi is a dedicated sophomore at Lamar University, majoring in Biology with a Chemistry minor and Pre-Med concentration. A fluent Arabic and English speaker from The Woodlands, Texas, he aspires to become a doctor in the medical field. Fun fact about Mohamed is that he has traveled to five out of the seven continents!

Morgan Irvine

Morgan Irvine is a graduate of Bridge City and currently a student at Lamar pursuing a major in English with a concentration in education and a minor in creative writing. Writing has always been a passion of hers and she often finds her inspiration from horror media and her own life.

Mitchell Junious

Mitchell A. Junious graduated from Lamar University's Communications department and currently studies writing in the English department's master's program. Before becoming employed at Lamar, where he directs and produces the ESPN+ broadcasts, he worked in the field of journalism, where he was awarded an Emmy© and recognized by the Texas Association of Broadcasters for his directing.

Gillian Laird

Gillian Laird is a young writer from Southeast Texas currently studying English at Lamar University. She has always harbored a deep passion for books and has been creatively writing for many years. Having been published in literary magazines such as *Pulse* and *Outrageous Fortune*, she plans to further pursue publication of her first novel after graduation.

Zoë Landers

Zoë Landers graduated from Lamar University with her Bachelors in English and is returning in Fall 2024 to earn her Masters. During the attainment of her undergraduate degree, she focused primarily on her short fiction works, but plans to spend her graduate degree further building her writing portfolio in longer form fiction and poetry.

Chad Le

Chad Le is an unassuming senior at Lamar University. He started writing poetry in middle school. Poetry was as an on-and-off avenue for personal thoughts and expression that continued throughout high school. While Chad does not write as much anymore, he still enjoys it and passes time with music, art, and sports.

Chloe Lopez

Chloe Lopez is a junior English major with a Psychology minor. She is an intern at Wesley, a student center dedicated to serving all, and a scholar in the 2024 Lamar University McNair Scholars Cohort. Chloe is also a member of Sigma Tau Delta, the English Honor Society. Outside of writing poetry, Lopez enjoys crocheting, bracelet making, spending time with her ragdoll cat, Riley, writing horror stories, and crafting.

Davonna Martin
Davonna Martin is a Junior at Lamar University, her major is studio art sculpture, and she lives in Beaumont, Texas. This is her second time submitting and being published to Pulse. With most of her poetry, she focuses on emotions that may be uncomfortable or relatable for others.

Raul Martin
Raul Martin IV graduated from Lamar University's Masters in English program in Fall 2023. He now serves his community as a full-time tutor and adjunct instructor at LSCO and LIT. His area of academic interest is the relationship between literature and the environment or ecocriticism. He lives in Vidor, Texas, with his wife.

Kaelee McCoy
Kaelee McCoy is a sophomore Psychology major and English minor from Vidor, TX. This is her first year at Lamar University, and her first publication in Pulse.

Kayla McKinley
Kayla McKinley is a freshman Exercise Science major with a concentration in Physical Therapy. She is not only a contributor for Pulse this year, but also for Cadenza, Lamar University's Reaud Honors College alumni magazine. She has been involved in various student organizations and this summer will be conducting research through Lamar University's SURF program. She is very honored and excited to share a short fictional story for publication in Pulse!

Marquis Moore
Marquis Moore is a creative individual who has a passion for art in various forms. He believes that art can bring people together and create a unique language of love. Whether through words, pictures, videos, thoughts, or a combination of all; he believes we can transform our minds and hearts to truly love one another.

Zachary Pruitt
Zachary is an English major with a minor in ASL from Bridge City, and has recently decided to pursue a career in audiology going forward. All of Zach's poetry is directly aligned with his faith and represent the struggle and joy that comes with following Christ.

Jarely Rebollar
Jarely Rebollar, a first-gen Mexican American from Beaumont, Texas, studies Psychology and Writing at Lamar University. After graduating

from Beaumont Early College High School, she hones her writing prowess through academics and extracurriculars. Passionate about education, she strives to excel in her pursuits, embodying resilience and cultural pride.

William Rowley

William Rowley is an English student at Lamar University. His love for classic horror and the study of the human experience inspires his own writing to focus on themes such as depression (namely men's mental health), nostalgia, romance, gothic horror, and body horror. Aside from writing fiction, he enjoys writing movie reviews, creating short films, and music.

Abigail Serrano

Abigail Serrano began her creative writing journey in elementary school when she had her children's book published. She continued creative writing throughout high school and published a book online. During her time at Lamar University, she had a short story published in the Pulse 2022-2023 issue, which encouraged her to expand her creative writing talent and write poetry.

Brandon Stumpf

Brandon is an undergraduate senior history major and English minor. He is a 2023-24 SURF research fellow at Lamar, and a board member on the Caroline Gilbert Hinchee House project in Beaumont. Brandon is currently working on a 2024-25 SURF research project involving Georgia courts in the American Antebellum South.

Darlene Thomas-Pierre

Darlene is a lover of words, writing poetry, prose, and sermonic pieces. She was formerly a contributing writer for the Urban Voice, which named her article, "Historical Society Fumbles on Port Arthur's History" as the Best History Article of the Year in 1999. Darlene is a senior Business major and McNair Scholar.

Jo Youngeun

Jo Youngeun is a graduate student in the Computer Science department. Through translating "The Widest Road," Youngeun hopes that all members of the university community can freely experience failure in the university experimental space and find their own 'Widest Road.'

Jeri Wolfe

Jeri Wolfe graduated from Lamar University in 2023 with a Bachelor of Arts in English. She is a free-time poet who aspires to be a journalist. She finds joy in crafting poems and stories that explore the human experience. Wolfe's poetic journey is a testament to her passion for language and highlights her goal to capture the nuances of life through words.

Pulse Staff

*Keely Viator — Chief Student Editor
Keely Viator is a graduate English major with a particular interest in both creative prose and poetry. She loves character development and reflection, and she may ramble about it if given the opportunity. She also likes to work her art into her storytelling when she has the energy to do so.

*Britton Larson — Poetry Editor
Britton Larson is a junior majoring in English at Lamar Unversity. He loves to read, particularly high fantasy fiction, and has recently enjoyed writing poetry as well. Britton enjoys working with Pulse as he gets to discover the writing talents of his fellow Cardinals.

*Claudia Cooper — Prose Editor
Claudia Cooper is an English major with a minor in creative writing. She has been Pulse's prose editor for two years and plans to make it a third. Claudia enjoys reading, writing, and annoying her friends whenever she has free time. Unfortunately for her friends, she has a lot of free time.

*Erica Callahan — Cover Artist
Erica is a freshman Civil Engineer at Lamar University. She enjoys reading, writing, doing art, and working on math in her spare time. She hopes to one day have enough money to make a home library. She would also like to look into publishing her writings one day.

*Christine Osborne — Technical and Design Editor
Christine Osborne is a graduate English major and works with the Literary Press as a graduate editor. She has recently re-acquired an affection for poetry and finds herself composing poems in the middle of mundane conversations. Christine enjoys reading, playing Call of Duty, and sewing in her free time, which is very often nonexistent.

Reilly Smith — Technical and Design Editor
Reilly Smith is a novice poet, a mother, and a graduate student of English at Lamar University. She works as an academic advisor for the Undergraduate Advising Center and enjoys working as a freelance editor in her spare time.

Mikaela Bartlett — Reader
Mikaela Bartlett is a freshman English major. She loves all things writing, reading, and editing, so being a reader for Pulse Literary Magazine felt like the perfect fit. She loved being exposed to poems with different voices, writing styles, and stories. She looks forward to experiencing new things through the English department and all that it offers!

Felix Campbell — Reader
Felix Campbell is a senior wrapping up their B.A in English degree. Being a writer himself, he is honored to be a part of the Pulse team this year. In the future, Felix aspires to be a creative writer, focusing on poetry and short fiction.

Isabella Deese — Reader
Isabella Deese is an aspiring novelist and poet who is currently pursuing an English degree at Lamar University. She is a lover of cats, plants, and the stars, and a hater of birds, denim, and khakis. She would like to melt into the sea one day, but until then she will continue to go to school and work at a local coffee shop.

Grace Harmon — Reader
Allison Grace Harmon (P.M.) is an undergraduate English major working as a student assistant within Lamar University's English Department. After her graduation in Spring of 2024, she intends to continue her education through the English Master's program. In her free time, she enjoys playing Skyrim and avoiding her deadlines.

Grace Nicholson — Reader
Grace Nicholson (A.M.) is a graduate student majoring in English. She is a self-proclaimed literature connoisseur who dabbles in writing and reading illegible poetry, fantasy fiction, and author biographies. She is the founder of the Society of English Mongrels, an unofficial graduate writing group for English Graduates at Lamar. She believes in wishing on stars and reading books that smell like book.

Savanna Peveto-Kreatschman — Reader
Savanna Peveto-Kreatschman is a Junior who is majoring in English and minoring in Writing. She loves reading, writing short stories, crocheting, and volunteering for the local dog shelter. In the future she hopes to have a Master's degree in Library Science and work at a Public Library.

Teri Wolfe — Reader

Teri Wolfe graduated Lamar University with a bachelor's degree in English, and she currently works in the Mary and John Gray Library. She has an interest in the arts—particularly writing, drawing, music, and theatre. While she likes to create her own works, she finds enjoyment in other people's creations and gets easily inspired from their contagious passion to create. She plans on further pursuing a master's degree in English as a fellow cardinal.

Lily Yoder — Reader

Lily Yoder graduated Lamar University with a bachelor's degree in psychology and a minor in writing and currently is pursuing an MA in English. She works in the department as a research and editorial assistant. She has an interest in creative writing, research, and academic writing, and enjoys reading her peers' creative and academic writing.

*These Pulse staff also contibuted poetry and/or prose to this edition.

www.ingramcontent.com/pod-product-compliance
Lightning Source LLC
Chambersburg PA
CBHW020617030726
47497CB00007B/2287